"Living in Palm Beach isn't all it's cracked up to be," Tina said.

"Or it wasn't until Sarah and Juliet and Mr. Kelly came along," she added. "They're real. They know all about loving and sharing and trust. *Some* of my neighbors love their stockbrokers more than they do their families."

"Are you including me in that group?" Drew asked.

"I'm not sure. After this afternoon I'm not sure anymore what you want from me."

He paused. "The answer's not so easy," he said at last. "You've awakened desires in me I've never felt before. I want to protect you and make love to you, but you've made it clear you don't want that."

Tina heard the raw edge of frustration in his voice. She wanted to believe he was telling the truth, but was it all of the truth, or only a convenient portion?

Dear Reader,

Sophisticated but sensitive, savvy yet unabashedly sentimental—that's today's woman, today's romance reader—you! And Silhouette Special Editions are written expressly to reward your quest for substantial, emotionally involving love stories.

So take a leisurely stroll under the cover's lavender arch into a garden of romantic delights. Pick and choose among titles if you must—we hope you'll soon equate all six Special Editions each month with consistently gratifying romantic reading.

Watch for sparkling new stories from your Silhouette favorites—Nora Roberts, Tracy Sinclair, Ginna Gray, Lindsay McKenna, Curtiss Ann Matlock, among others—along with some exciting newcomers to Silhouette, such as Karen Keast and Patricia Coughlin. Be on the lookout, too, for the new Silhouette Classics, a distinctive collection of bestselling Special Editions and Silhouette Intimate Moments now brought back to the stands—two each month—by popular demand.

On behalf of all the authors and editors of Special Editions,
Warmest wishes,

Leslie Kazanjian
Senior Editor

SHERRYL WOODS
Safe Harbor

Silhouette Special Edition

Published by Silhouette Books New York

America's Publisher of Contemporary Romance

SILHOUETTE BOOKS
300 East 42nd St., New York, N.Y. 10017

Copyright © 1987 by Sherryl Woods

ISBN: 0-373-09425-6

First Silhouette Books printing December 1987

America's Publisher of Contemporary Romance

Printed in the U.S.A.

Books by Sherryl Woods

Silhouette Desire

Not at Eight, Darling #309
Yesterday's Love #329
Come Fly with Me #345
A Gift of Love #375

Silhouette Special Edition

Safe Harbor #425

SHERRYL WOODS

lives by the ocean, which provides daily inspiration for the romance in her soul. Her years as a television critic taught her about steamy plots and humor. Her years as a travel editor took her to exotic locations. Her years as a crummy weekend tennis player taught her to stick with what she enjoyed most: writing. What better way to combine all of that than by writing romantic stories about wonderful heroines, sensitive heroes and enchanting locations?

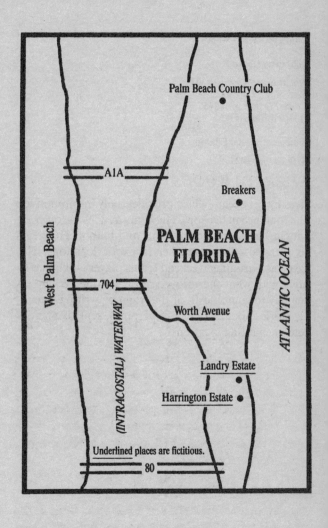

Palm Beach Country Club

Breakers

PALM BEACH FLORIDA

A1A

704

Worth Avenue

Landry Estate

Harrington Estate

West Palm Beach

(INTRACOSTAL) WATERWAY

ATLANTIC OCEAN

Underlined places are fictitious.

80

Chapter One

It had all started with Sam.

That was it, Tina decided, throwing herself into one of the antique wicker chairs overlooking the pool and perfectly landscaped terrace. The palm trees with their limply hanging branches seemed to reflect her mood perfectly as she stared dolefully at the thick vellum papers in her hand. She only barely resisted the urge to crumple them up and throw them for one of the cats to bat around the lawn, possibly straight into the pool's sparkling turquoise water. It would be a fitting end to the documents. As for her bad habit, it seemed there was no end in sight.

It had all started twenty years ago, back when she was eight and that scrawny marmalade kitten she'd named Sam had made its way to her front door. It had meowed so pitifully that not even her father had been able to resist Tina's pleas to take it in. Ever since then, she'd been adopting strays.

Sam had been followed by Penelope, the gerbil who was about to be sent away to who-knew-what awful fate by her best friend, then by Sam's totally unexpected litter of kittens. Bandit, who barked as though he had laryngitis, had limped in with a thorn in his front paw and stayed for nearly ten years, bringing home friends when it suited him.

By the time she'd left for the University of Florida, the house had looked like a damned menagerie, according to her amazingly tolerant parents. They might not have known where the next mortgage payment was coming from, but they'd always found room in their hearts and food scraps for one more of Tina's pets.

They should see me now, she thought with a sigh as she reread the letter from the Florida Department of Health and Rehabilitative Services. The letter was filled with legal jargon, but what it boiled down to was an accusation that she was taking in human strays without benefit of a license, followed by a stern admonition that she should cease and desist promptly or risk penalties meant to scare the daylights out of her. The threats only infuriated her.

She glared at the paper. Those pompous, meddling fools! Of all the ridiculous, simpleminded ...

"Tina, dear, I've brought you a nice glass of iced tea," Grandmother Sarah said as she set down a tall, frosted glass, then sat herself and waved a lilac-scented, lace-edged hankie to stir the still, humid air into a slight breeze. "My, but it's a scorcher today. I'll be so glad when we get another cold front through here to cool things off."

"The minute the temperature goes below seventy you complain that your arthritis acts up," Tina reminded her with a gently teasing smile.

"Posh-tosh. My arthritis acts up all the time. I'm an old lady."

"Some days I think you're younger than I am," Tina said with a heavy sigh that drew a sharp-eyed glance from Grandmother Sarah.

Grandmother Sarah, with her wisps of flyaway white hair surrounding a weathered face, her sparkling periwinkle blue eyes and her flowered print dress, wasn't Tina's grandmother at all. They had met a year ago while walking on the beach and had started talking. It hadn't taken long for the gregarious and unceasingly curious Tina to discover that the spirited, elderly woman with her spry manner and tart tongue was about to be thrown out of her soon-to-be-demolished rooming house and had nowhere to live. She'd invited Sarah home as casually as she'd admitted Sam all those years ago. She hadn't regretted the spontaneous suggestion for a single minute. It had been like she'd always imagined having a real grandmother would be.

Tina gazed at Grandmother Sarah fondly and took a long swallow of the cool drink. The way she was feeling, it probably should have been a mint julep at the very least. Maybe even straight bourbon. If the ominous tone of the letter she held was any indication, she had a feeling she was in for the fight of her life.

Intuitive as always, Sarah picked up on her mood.

"Dear, if you don't mind my saying so, you look a mite peaked. Is it the weather or is something wrong?"

Tina shook her head.

Grandmother Sarah regarded her critically. "Your nose is growing, child. Fibbing is not becoming."

"I didn't say a word."

"Exactly."

"Okay, there is a problem. But it's nothing for you to worry about."

Sarah's eyes narrowed and she retorted spiritedly, "Of course it is. I'm your friend, aren't I? If something has you all in a tizzy, then the rest of us certainly want to help."

Tina didn't have the heart to explain that the rest of them *were* the problem. Grandmother Sarah was only the tip of the iceberg. There was slightly dotty Aunt Juliet, also no relation, as well as little Billy and old Mr. Kelly, to say nothing of Sam's great-grandchildren, one of Bandit's descendants and Lady MacBeth, a parrot who had the vocabulary of a drunken sailor.

No matter how she looked at it, Tina admitted, it was not your typical household. But that didn't mean she was breaking the law, although clannish, well-moneyed Palm Beach seemed to have a whole encyclopedia of etiquette and a long list of specialized zoning regulations all its own.

It had been five years now, but she'd never quite gotten used to the transition she'd made from her barely middle class childhood in West Palm Beach to the wealthy island enclave across the bridge. Her three-year marriage to Gerald Harrington had given her instantaneous social status, financial security, an estate that edged the Atlantic Ocean and, most of all, a joyous, storybook love.

Gerald's accidental death in the crash of the company jet two years earlier had devastated her. At twenty-six, she was left rattling around in a huge old house, surrounded by servants who refused to even sit down and play a card game with her. They put her meals on the table, then retreated to await the tinkle of a bell. The cook would have been horrified if she'd known that Tina would have preferred to eat in the kitchen. The butler would have been equally shocked if she'd suggested he join her at the imposing dining room table. As a result of their stuffy sense of station, she'd been faced with an intolerable loneliness at the end of every long, tiring day she spent at Harrington Industries.

Then a year ago, just when she'd thought things were at their bleakest, Grandmother Sarah, Aunt Juliet and the rest had come along needing the kind of assistance and friendship she could easily offer. Now she felt as though her life were worth living again. No one was going to take that away from her.

"You got another one of those letters, didn't you?" Grandmother Sarah said, her sharp gaze falling on the paper that Tina had tossed defiantly on the table.

"Yes," she admitted, reluctantly conceding that there was no point in denying the obvious.

"Who's this one from?"

"The state."

"My, my. He is pulling out the big guns, isn't he?"

He, of course, was Drew Landry, her new neighbor and the man behind this letter and a whole series that had preceded it. The man was attacking her way of life with tactical efforts worthy of a marine commander and the persistence of a pit bull.

"I just don't understand it," Tina muttered. "What difference could it possibly make to Drew Landry if I have a few houseguests?"

Grandmother Sarah lifted her eyebrows. "Okay," Tina muttered defensively. "So you're not exactly houseguests in the traditional sense. You didn't drop in from Monte Carlo or London or Boston. You're not just here for the annual Red Cross Gala. I still don't see what business it is of his or the State of Florida."

"Why don't you talk to him, dear? Explain about all of this. I'm sure he's a reasonable man."

An image of Drew Landry flashed in Tina's mind. Her tall, dark, jet-setting neighbor with the formidable scowl and the well-toned, impressively proportioned body struck her as anything but reasonable. On the one occasion when they'd met, long enough for her to offer to pay for the window Billy had broken with the best-hit ball of his Little League career, Landry's extraordinary blue eyes had flashed angrily, the nostrils of his patrician nose had flared and his full, sensuous lips emitted a string of oaths her parrot would have envied. Tina, who was rarely intimidated, had literally quaked under the impact of his fury. It was not a scene she was anxious to repeat.

"I don't think talking to Mr. Landry will accomplish a thing. He seems pretty set in his ways."

"Fiddlesticks! How can a thirty-seven-year-old man be set in his ways?" Grandmother Sarah argued.

Tina shot her a startled look. "How do you know how old he is?"

"I read the papers. He's been in the gossip columns nearly every day since he got to town." She gave Tina a sly, assessing glance. "Quite a hunk, if you ask me."

"A hunk?" Tina snorted derisively. "Looks aren't everything, you know."

"Oh, I know that well enough, but if you ask me, you could use a hunk in your life. It's time you put Gerald behind you and got on with things. Juliet and I were discussing it just the other night. You're far too young to be shut away here with only us old folks for company."

"Billy's only thirteen," she reminded Sarah, "and my social life is just fine, thank you very much."

"If you're into—what's the word you use all the time about some of your lily-livered board members—wimps."

Tina's brown eyes flashed, but she couldn't put much spirit into her defense. "Martin is a very successful man. He is not a wimp."

"He does a fine job of impersonating one," Sarah declared. "How can you say that man's successful? He's living on his daddy's money. I'll bet he's never gone out and earned a dime himself. And the way he dresses..." She shook her head sadly. "I'll bet that man has never once gotten his hands dirty. Now what kind of a man is that?"

"We are not talking about Martin," Tina retorted in exasperation. She'd heard Sarah's opinions of her companion often enough. "We're talking about Drew Landry and his ridiculous notion that we're destroying his property value or something. He just bought the place three months ago, for heaven's sakes. He hardly needs to worry about the selling price now."

"What makes you think he's worried about his property value?"

"What other reason could he have for meddling in something that's none of his business?"

"I have no idea, but I still say you ought to talk to him and find out. You could settle this thing once and for all," Sarah suggested with a sudden gleam in her eyes. Tina eyed her nervously and waited for the rest. It didn't take long.

"In fact," Sarah said, "why don't you go over right this minute and invite him for dinner tonight? I'll bake one of my cherry pies. There's not a man alive who can resist warm cherry pie topped with homemade vanilla ice cream."

"Drew Landry strikes me as the type who'd only appreciate Cherries Jubilee and champagne."

Grandmother Sarah was obstinate as a mule. "I'm telling you, the cherry pie will do it. Go on, Christina Elizabeth," she persisted in her very best grandmotherly, don't-cross-me tone. "Before you lose your nerve."

"Lose it?" Tina muttered as she reluctantly set off across the sweeping lawn. "I don't have any nerve to lose. The man scares me out of my wits."

Then she thought about the stakes, about Sarah and Juliet and Billy and Mr. Kelly, to say nothing of the assorted pets, and a tiny flare of anger sparked to life in the pit of her stomach. She fanned it for all she was worth. By the time she'd slipped through a widening in the hedge—when Gerald had been a boy, his best friend had lived next door—she was ready to make Drew Landry rue the day he'd ever set out to destroy her perfectly happy if somewhat unorthodox household.

The gray-haired, tight-lipped butler who answered the door was so stiff she was afraid he'd shatter if he cracked a smile. He definitely was not the type to settle down and spend an evening playing gin rummy. She wondered if he and the man she'd finally fired, along with the cook, were related. They'd clearly been turned out of the same mold.

His narrowed eyes took in her skimpy, one-piece sunsuit with the bright purple flowers on a turquoise background and he virtually sniffed his disapproval. She was surprised he didn't ask her to go around to the kitchen entrance.

"Mr. Landry is on the terrace, miss. If you'll follow me." It was less a suggestion than a command. Tina obeyed, trying to control a practically irresistible urge to giggle.

Even after five years in Palm Beach, during which she'd grown accustomed to the often ridiculous dictums of high society, it had never ceased to amaze her that the servants were sometimes even stuffier and more class conscious than their bosses. She'd seen chauffeurs stand by the family Mercedes or Cadillac or Lincoln on Worth Avenue and look down their haughty noses at each other, while their mistresses shopped in elegant boutiques or lunched together in fancy restaurants.

She didn't have time to explore this social phenomenon too closely because she was suddenly on the terrace. Mr. Landry was not sipping tea and eating fresh scones or using a portable phone to make million-dollar business deals as she'd half expected. Instead, he was swimming laps in a pool that curved like a lagoon amid an abundance of palm trees and bright yellow hibiscus. Her breath caught in her throat as she watched his lean, tanned body slice through the sparkling water with practiced ease, creating hardly a ripple... except along her spine, which she instinctively straightened in the hope the sensation would go away. It didn't.

Tina barely noticed when the butler left. Her eyes traveled slowly from the shoulders that glistened in the late afternoon sun, taking in the muscles that moved with sleek grace, the long legs that kicked with controlled power. A wayward image of those legs tangling with her own in the heat of passion ripped into her mind creating a feverish tension. She sighed softly.

As the annoyingly wistful whisper of sound escaped, Drew Landry swam to the side of the pool and gazed straight into her eyes, the knowing cobalt blue of his taunting her as he lifted himself out of the water and stood before her like someone waiting to be admired.

The disarray of his damp black hair caught the sparks of afternoon sunlight like coal turned to diamonds. Rivulets of water ran down his muscled torso, lingered in the dark hairs that were matted on his chest, then continued over his flat stomach to be captured by the band of a barely decent, skin-hugging bathing suit. Tina was fascinated by those trails of water, her pulse beating ever faster as her gaze followed their path, then froze on that skimpy piece of material.

"Is there something you wanted?" The lazy drawl was filled with amused innuendo.

Tina shook her head, meeting laughing eyes.

"I mean yes," she mumbled, fighting embarrassment and a disturbing desire to run a finger along the tempting path created by that trail of water. She was not going to let Drew Landry have the upper hand for even a split second. She certainly was going to keep her hands to herself. She jammed them into her pockets, just to be sure.

"We have to talk," she said in the firm, decisive voice she'd trained herself to use when she wanted to tactfully persuade the board of directors of Harrington Industries to heed her advice.

Drew Landry lazily rubbed a towel over his awesome body, and Tina forced herself to look at the branch of lovely pale lavender orchids hanging from a tree just beyond his shoulder. In the end, though, she couldn't resist sneaking just one more peak. Grandmother Sarah was right. He was a hunk.

"We do?" he said skeptically. "Am I supposed to know why?"

"You're trying to destroy my family. I want to know what you're up to."

"My dear Mrs. Harrington..."

"So, then, you do remember me?"

He grinned, and her heart lurched in what had to be an infuriatingly Pavlovian reaction.

"How could I forget?" he was saying when she finally managed to concentrate. "Our first meeting was rather...inauspicious."

She gazed at him sharply. "You say that as though I were some sort of criminal you'd caught stealing the family silver. It was only a kitchen window, for heaven's sakes, and Billy didn't mean to do it."

"The window is forgotten. I'm more concerned with what you're doing to those poor people, to say nothing of the neighborhood. It's nothing short of criminal. My God, woman, you can't turn your home into a refuge for all the derelicts in the world. There are zoning laws, to say nothing of state regulations about that sort of thing."

"The laws are absurd and they don't apply anyway."

"The zoning laws may be ridiculous, but they exist nonetheless. As for the state regulations, they are designed to protect innocent people, no matter their background, from cranks."

"I am hardly a crank, and my friends are not derelicts," she replied heatedly. "They may have had a rough time, but they're honest, kind, wonderful people."

"Are they members of your family?"

"You mean legally?"

He grinned again, a dimple on his left cheek teasing her. Her traitorous heart skipped several beats.

"That's generally the way it works," he said dryly. "Either by birth or marriage."

Captivated by the slow caress of the towel over his masculine body, Tina had trouble remembering the original question. She forced herself to concentrate on the conversation. Families. They'd been talking about families and whether she was related to Grandmother Sarah and the others.

"No. Of course not," she admitted at last, then added defiantly, "That doesn't mean I love them any less."

"Perhaps not. But it does mean they have no business living there, unless you can get a license to operate a congregate living facility."

"A congregate living facility?" she repeated in astonishment. "Is that what you think I'm doing?"

"Isn't it? How many nonfamily members do you have tucked away in the corners of that mansion of yours? Or can you even find them all?"

She shot him a scathing glare. "There are only three." She paused. "Well, four, if you count Billy, but he's only a child."

He seemed taken aback for the moment. He'd obviously thought there were dozens. "It's still three or four too many if they're not related," he finally said.

"Tell me," she said sarcastically, "is old Giles in there...?"

"Giles?"

"Giles. Henry. Whatever his name is. Your butler. Is he a member of your family?"

"Of course not, and his name is Geoffrey."

"Then I fail to see the difference."

"He's an employee."

She nodded sagely. "I see. You pay him, so that entitles him to live here. I don't pay my friends to live with me, so that's illegal. Have I got this down yet?"

"You're missing the point," he retorted impatiently, the grin fading. Her heart jolted one more time just the same. The reaction was getting downright irritating. You'd think she'd never seen a practically nude man before. Why didn't he put some clothes on?

She glared up at him. It was an incredibly long distance, even for her, and she was a taller-than-average five-foot-eight. Once her eyes met his, she was almost sorry she'd bothered. His dark eyes were very distracting, suggesting hidden depths and tantalizing mysteries. What was wrong with her? Was it possible to get sunstroke from a five-minute walk?

She forced her mind to seize yet another point that had been about to drift away and lashed back at him. "I'm not missing the point. You are. These people are my guests."

"Guests?" he repeated skeptically. "Are you trying to tell me you don't charge those poor souls to live there?"

"Mr. Landry!" Her voice rose and this time she had absolutely no trouble staring disdainfully into his obnoxious, doubting eyes. She drew herself up to her full height and, despite her casual attire, managed to look every bit the corporate executive she was.

"My late husband built Harrington Industries into one of the top corporations in the country. Perhaps you've heard of it?" She regarded him questioningly. He nodded, his lips twitching with amusement. She continued, "I inherited that when he died. I have an M.B.A., take an active role in the day-to-day operation of the company and am chairman of the board. Our profits have doubled in the last two years. Our stock, of which I own a significant percentage, has tripled. Do you honestly think I need to earn extra pocket money by taking in boarders?"

He studied her curiously, as if he'd just discovered an alien creature on his lawn and was trying to understand its strange language. "Then why do you do it?"

"Because I like them, Mr. Landry. My parents are dead. I don't have a lot of family left in the world and the ones who are left tend to want the fortune I inherited, rather than my affection. On the other hand, the people who stay with me don't give a hang about the balance in my checking account. They buy the groceries when they can afford to. Grandmother Sarah cooks. Aunt Juliet does my correspondence, and Mr. Kelly tends to the lawn and the garden. Billy does his share of the chores, too."

"So they're servants, then. Why didn't you just say so?"

Tina stamped her foot, a purely feminine reaction that was so out of character it astonished her. The man was destroying her reason. The next thing she knew she'd be bursting into tears like some simpering female. She steeled herself against that awful possibility.

"You just don't see it, do you?" she snapped back. "They are not my servants. They are not my boarders. They are my friends, and you and your expensive legal eagles are not about to break up my home, if I have to go to court and adopt every last one of them."

She whirled around and started toward the house, then turned back and met his still-puzzled gaze. "By the way, Grandmother Sarah wants you to come to dinner tonight. God knows why, but she thinks you might like her homemade cherry pie."

"And you?"

"I think you're too damned pompous to want to eat with some people you obviously consider your inferiors."

"I'll be there at eight."

Tina stared at him in astonishment. He wasn't supposed to agree. He was supposed to laugh in her face. Maybe Grandmother Sarah was right after all. Maybe the man was a sucker for cherry pie. She noted the disconcerting gleam in his eyes as they traveled over the swell of her breasts and down to her long, slender legs, which were revealed all too enticingly by the sunsuit. She should have worn a demure silk suit and a strand of pearls. Instead, she hadn't even worn shoes. Her toes curled against the cool tiles on the shaded side of the terrace.

"Make it seven," she said at last. "Aunt Juliet goes to bed early and, if she eats too late, it upsets her stomach and keeps her up all night."

He chuckled and the sound washed over her like a cooling afternoon shower. It made her feel good. It should have made her feel rotten, she told herself stoutly. In fact, she shouldn't be affected at all. The insufferable Mr. Landry was not deserving of one more instant's worth of worry or consideration. He certainly should not be stirring up her blood this way.

She tried telling herself that again when she was soaking in scented bubble bath, and once more when she was dressing in a bright yellow cotton sundress that bared her creamy shoulders and nipped in at her tiny waist. She repeated the statement as she uncoiled her auburn hair and let it fall to her shoulders in a temple tangle of curls. As she touched her cheeks with blusher and swept a coral lipstick over her full, sensuous lips, which always looked as though they'd just been kissed, she murmured it aloud at her reflection in the mirror.

"You look lovely, dear," Grandmother Sarah noted with a satisfied smile when Tina walked into the kitchen.

"Oh my, yes," Aunt Juliet concurred. Mr. Kelly whistled approvingly.

"This Landry guy must be something special, huh?" Billy said, winking at Grandmother Sarah, who winked right back. "She never looks like this when Martin's coming over."

"Like what?" Tina said, looking down at her simple dress, which she'd bought off the rack at a sale a week before. She'd thought she was dressing down for the occasion. They were acting like she'd gone on a designer binge and outfitted herself for a date with somebody really important, instead of a meal at home with a man she didn't even like.

"Sexy," Bill responded. Grandmother Sarah and Aunt Juliet nodded enthusiastic agreement.

"Absolutely perfect. He won't be able to resist you," Grandmother Sarah gushed.

"Damn it!" Tina muttered. "What is wrong with all of you? I am not interested in Drew Landry. I am only interested in ending this ridiculous vendetta of his."

"Of course you are, dear," Grandmother Sarah said, and patted her hand consolingly. Aunt Juliet, who was as romantic as her namesake, chuckled delightedly, and Billy left the room whistling an off-key version of "Here Comes the Bride."

Tina wondered if maybe Drew Landry weren't right after all. Maybe she should toss these people straight out on their ears.

Except, perhaps, for Mr. Kelly. He was very good with the garden, and his huge, home-grown tomatoes were sinfully delicious. She couldn't give those up.

As for the rest, they were flat-out meddling.

Just like family, she thought with a sigh.

Chapter Two

When the doorbell rang just as the grandfather clock in the hallway chimed seven, Tina jumped nervously and began whipping the potatoes with enough force to stir concrete. She was hoping that one of the other people who lived in the house would have enough sense to answer the door, leaving her in the kitchen where she'd be safely out of Drew Landry's sight...perhaps until after dessert had been served. If Grandmother Sarah was right, he'd be in a much more amenable mood by then. She doubted if he'd be any less intimidating.

She'd discovered this afternoon that the man didn't just scare her to death because of his temper. He also attracted her in a purely male-female sort of way that had been so totally unexpected it made her very nervous. She did not think a rational woman would be drawn to a man who'd been demonstrating the compassion and single-mindedness of a steamroller. Never in her life had she met anyone who could stir her anger and her blood at the same time. Drew Landry's bold arrogance infuriated her, yet she couldn't deny that he also stirred her heartbeat to a wild, exciting tempo. The conspiratorial matchmaking that seemed to be going on around the house tonight, and the all-too-knowing hints about her own intentions toward Drew Landry, hadn't done a thing to calm her nerves. She felt like an aging spinster faced with an unwanted blind date and surrounded by a hopeful family that was inclined to prod her toward the altar no matter the suitability of the man.

The doorbell chimed again, and this time Grandmother Sarah gave her a penetrating look. "Aren't you going to get the door, dear?"

"I'm in the middle of fixing the potatoes. Maybe Mr. Kelly..."

"He went back upstairs to change. His clothes were covered with mud from the garden."

"Billy, then."

"Do you think that's wise? I mean he did break the man's window. It might get the evening off to a bad start. I could go, but the pies..."

"Oh, darn," Tina muttered grumpily. "I'll get the door."

"Remember to smile, dear. You can catch more flies with honey than you can with vinegar."

"Does the same hold true for a snake?"

"Tina!"

"Oh, I know," she said with a sigh. "I'll be nice to the man. Just remember when this whole thing blows up in our faces that this was your idea."

Sarah chose to ignore the gibe. "Be sure to offer him a drink. A man's always more receptive after he's had a nice drink to soothe his nerves."

"Should I offer to give him a massage, too?"

"Tina!" This time Sarah, who could feign the Southern gentlewoman, sounded properly scandalized, and Tina felt guilty right down to her toes.

"Sorry. I was just joking."

The impatient chiming of the doorbell for the third time sent Tina scurrying down the hall through the tiled foyer to the door. She swung it open to find Drew Landry glaring at the magnificent, intricately carved wood with its stained-glass inserts as though it personally were responsible for holding him up. It was too much to hope that he would have gotten angry and left.

"Am I too early?"

From Tina's point of view, the twenty-first century would have been too early, however she said only, "No. Of course not. I was in the kitchen."

"Oh?" He lifted his brows with an infuriating expression of skepticism that made her want to stamp her foot again—right on top of his. "Cook's night off?"

Amber eyes immediately sparked with anger. Talk about getting things off to a bad start. "I don't have a cook," she said stiffly. "Nor do I have a butler. As I explained this afternoon, we do our own work around here."

"How very democratic of you."

She studied him curiously. "Are you always such a stuffed shirt?"

Blue eyes bored into her, and suddenly a grin appeared on his very sensuous mouth. Kissing that mouth could prove to be very exciting, she decided thoughtfully.

And absurdly dangerous, she added very quickly.

"Straightforward thing, aren't you?" he said, and she knew it wasn't exactly meant as a compliment. She smiled at him cheerfully anyway.

"I try to be."

"Do you suppose I could come in, or do you want me to dine out here?"

"Actually I could send Aunt Juliet out with a plate," Tina said after thoughtful consideration.

He shook his head with greatly exaggerated sorrow. "Mrs. Harrington, I'm truly sorry."

Tina stared at him, thoroughly puzzled by his unexpectedly sympathetic tone. "About what?"

"Your failure to graduate from finishing school."

"I didn't go to finishing school."

"Ah. That explains it, then."

"Explains what?"

"Your unorthodox manners."

At that, Tina did blush. Her parents might have grown up on the wrong side of the tracks by Drew Landry's high and mighty standards, but they would have been horrified by her behavior. For that matter, so would Grandmother Sarah and Aunt Juliet. She had invited the man to dinner, even if it had been against her better judgment. Now that he was here in her home—or on her doorstep to be more precise—she was behaving like an ill-mannered, spoiled brat.

"I'm the one who's sorry, Mr. Landry. Please," she said, holding the door open. "Come in."

She led him into the living room, which was the one room in the stately old house that she absolutely hated. It still had heavy, burgundy velvet drapes, dark Oriental carpets and solid antique furniture that was totally out of keeping with the airy, tropical Florida setting and the rambling, Spanish-style house. It had been Gerald's favorite room, though, and, while he'd allowed her to do as she pleased with the rest of the house, he'd remained adamant about keeping this room the way it was. He'd told her once that it reminded him of his grandparents' home in Boston. Because of that sentimental tie she hadn't yet been able to bring herself to redecorate in a style more suited to her own informal taste.

"What a charming room," Drew said, his gaze lingering on the mahogany bookshelves lined with expensively bound volumes of the classics. Either he had borderline taste, Tina thought, or he had gone to finishing school and passed the elementary course in polite chitchat that she'd missed.

"Isn't it?" chimed in a whispery, disembodied feminine voice.

"Aunt Juliet?" Tina said, instantly on guard. "Where are you?"

"Over here," the voice replied.

"Over where?"

"Behind the drapes."

Tina sighed. Apparently it was going to be another one of Aunt Juliet's less than conventional nights. "Why?"

Sparkling brown eyes, peering out from behind wire-rimmed glasses that had slipped to the end of a pert nose, appeared at the edge of the drapes. "I was watching for Mr. Kelly."

"Mr. Kelly is upstairs."

"Oh," Aunt Juliet said, sighing in disappointment. "I was so hoping to see him tonight."

"You will see him, Aunt Juliet," Tina said patiently, wondering just what Drew was going to make of this scene. She and the rest of the household had gotten used to Aunt Juliet's whimsical departures from reality, but to an outsider already expecting the worst she must seem decidedly odd. "He'll be down for dinner shortly."

"Oh, good," Juliet said happily, slipping into the room and catching sight of Drew. She tilted her head at an inquisitive angle to get a better look at him and smoothed her sedate black dress down over her ample figure. Aunt Juliet had dressed in mourning since her own husband's death thirty-five years earlier, and not even Tina's gaily-colored Christmas and birthday offerings had been able to tempt her out of her somber attire. The gifts were still hanging in Juliet's closet. Now she touched her fingers lightly to the wisps of fading brown hair that were escaping from the braided coil on top of her head.

"And who is this?" she asked, staring at Drew with interest.

"This is Mr. Landry, Aunt Juliet. You remember, we invited him for dinner."

"Well, of course I remember. I'm not senile yet," she grumbled. "How do you do, Mr. Landry? Tina has told us so much about you."

"Really?"

"Yes. I'm sure you'll be very happy together. Tina is such a lovely girl. We're all quite fond of her."

Tina choked and tried to think of some urgent crisis that might require her immediate attention. Unfortunately, the only crisis seemed to be right here. She glanced sideways at Drew to see how he was taking the unexpected announcement of their betrothal. His gaze was sliding over her, an appreciative gleam building in his eyes, an amused quirk playing about his lips. He looked satisfied.

"Yes, she is lovely," he said, taking her hand and bringing it to those lips. They were just as soft, just as sensuously persuasive as she'd imagined. In fact, their touch was so disturbing that Tina wanted to jerk her hand away, but he was holding it with just enough pressure to prevent her from doing it. His mouth caressed the back of her hand, then the inside of her wrist, and currents of awareness ripped unexpectedly through her like an unexpected bolt of lightning. She had the oddest sensation that the storm between them was beginning and that it was destined to be a wildly passionate one.

"A drink," she mumbled, working her hand loose from his grasp as she caught the despicable, knowing laughter in his eyes. "Aunt Juliet, would you like some sherry?"

"That would be lovely."

"Mr. Landry?"

"Scotch, please."

"With water? Soda?"

"No. Straight, on the rocks."

Naturally he'd want it straight, she thought as she went to the bar. Frankly, she wouldn't mind a straight swallow of the stuff herself, she thought, noting that if today had been any indication, the man definitely seemed to have the potential to drive her to drink. The thought held a definite appeal. Maybe then, with a strong drink under her belt, she wouldn't notice that her hand was still shaking or that there was an intense, white-hot sensation settling low in her abdomen.

Martin, damn him, had never stirred such feelings in her, she thought with an irrational surge of fury. Come to think of it, Martin had never kissed her hand. He'd settled for ending each date with a chaste peck on the cheek.

Much as she hated to admit it, Grandmother Sarah was probably right about Martin. He wasn't the right man for her. Not after Gerald. They might share the same social circle and the same interests, but her evenings with him were less exciting than the ones she spent playing cutthroat Scrabble with Mr. Kelly and Aunt Juliet.

Already she knew that Drew Landry was definitely more exciting than a Scrabble game. He would never settle for a chaste peck on the cheek. The man was as bold and greedy as a pirate. His lips would maraud hers, his tongue plundering her mouth for every wildly stirring sensation.

As she handed him his drink and caught the predatory gleam in his eye once again, she knew that he would accept nothing less than total possession. The thought, complete with more of those enticingly sensual images, sent a shudder through her. Her brain obviously had not been speaking to her body lately. Otherwise her hormones would not be reacting with such ridiculous abandon to a man that she'd already ascertained was a domineering, class-conscious jerk, out to ruin her life and send her dearest friends packing.

Dinner, she decided, was going to be very interesting. The whole evening was potentially explosive. If the first few minutes were anything to go by, it was also going to seem interminably long.

She decided to leave Drew alone with Aunt Juliet and try to hurry dinner along. Excusing herself, she raced back to the kitchen.

"Is it ready yet?"

"Another few minutes," Sarah said. "How is it going?"

"Aunt Juliet is entertaining him."

Sarah's eyebrows lifted. "Oh, my. Perhaps you should get back."

"Don't worry. She can't do much more harm. She's already informed him that she thinks we'll be very happy together."

Sarah brightened. "That's wonderful. I must admit the thought had crossed my mind, too."

"Oh, for heaven's sakes. You don't even know the man," Tina grumbled. "Will you stop matchmaking and get dinner on the table. I want him out of here."

"Dear, he just arrived, and the whole point of this evening is to show him that he doesn't have to worry about having us for neighbors."

"I think we've already lost that argument. Aunt Juliet was hiding behind the drapes when he arrived."

Sarah shrugged. "He can't possibly make too much out of that. Now if she'd been running through the neighborhood naked..."

Tina shuddered. "Don't even say it."

"Christina, you know perfectly well I was only trying to make a point. Juliet is a lady. She would never do that," Sarah huffed indignantly. She paused thoughtfully. "And I don't think Mr. Kelly is likely to do it anymore, either. He loves those new pajamas you gave him after the first time he went for a midnight stroll in the altogether."

"Thank goodness we stopped him from sleepwalking before he got off the estate."

"No," Sarah chided. "Thank goodness we caught him before he caught his death of cold running around in the middle of the night."

She dished up a bowl of Mr. Kelly's fresh green beans and handed them to Tina. "Put these on the table, dear, and then call everyone. Dinner's ready."

Tina got Billy and Mr. Kelly first, then went back to the living room for Drew and Aunt Juliet. She found them bent over the Scrabble board.

"There is no such word, Mr. Landry," Aunt Juliet was protesting vehemently.

"Of course, there is. You're just mad because I got to use my *q* and my *x* in the same word with double points," he teased.

"Mr. Landry don't you try to cheat an old lady. *Quick* does not have an *x* in it."

His brow creased in a frown, and he gazed at her uncertainly. Only Tina caught the gently teasing laughter in his eyes. "Are you sure?"

"It's a good thing you're an executive," Juliet consoled.

"Oh? Why is that?"

"So you can hire a secretary to spell for you."

Drew laughed heartily at the sharp retort. To Tina's amazement, he actually seemed to be having a good time. In fact, he didn't seem the least bit stuffy, which was more than a little disconcerting. She could fight an attraction to a man who disapproved of her friends. She wasn't at all sure she could do battle with a man who was fitting in like one of the family.

"I must have been thinking of *quixotic*," he said, casting a significant glance at Tina, who scowled back at him.

"I may be a bit idealistic, but I am also very practical, Mr. Landry," Tina said. "That's why I'd like to invite you to come to dinner before it gets cold."

"Is Mr. Kelly there?" Aunt Juliet inquired in a whisper to Tina.

Tina grinned at her. From the moment that Jacob Kelly had moved in, Aunt Juliet had been smitten. So far, though, her love had gone unrequited. "He's there."

"Do I look okay?"

"You look positively lovely," Drew chimed in, gallantly offering her his arm. "Let's go make this Mr. Kelly of yours insanely jealous. Perhaps we should tell him that I've made you a proposal of marriage and that you're seriously considering it."

Aunt Juliet giggled like a schoolgirl and blushed becomingly. "Why, Mr. Landry, you devil. You know perfectly well you're much too young for an old woman like me. Besides, whatever would Tina think?"

He gazed over at Tina, his blue eyes warmly appraising, and her heart turned another somersault.

"Oh, I don't think she'd mind loaning me out to a friend just this once. Would you, dear?"

"Of course not, *dear*," she retorted sweetly, then wondered if she'd feel quite so charitable if the friend were thirty and gorgeous, instead of a slightly faded, if charming seventy-two. It was probably a question best left unanswered.

In the dining room, Tina performed the introductions and tried to ignore the way Grandmother Sarah was openly assessing Drew and nodding approvingly. Clearly, if things were to be left up to her, Tina's fate would be sealed. Aunt Juliet might have made a slightly dazed miscalculation about the relationship between Tina and her guest, but Sarah was sound of mind and very quick. She was perfectly capable of launching a series of romantic maneuvers that would land Tina and Drew in front of a minister before brunch next Sunday. Since Drew had no way of knowing what he was up against, it was up to Tina to dodge Sarah's carefully planned snares.

She missed the first one.

No sooner had she been seated in her usual place than Sarah was nudging Billy away from his regular chair on her left and urging Drew toward it. The quickly executed maneuver put Drew's long legs within mere inches of Tina's. In fact, if she shifted only slightly toward the radiating heat of his flesh, their knees would be touching. She had the darnedest urge to slip her foot out of its sandal and run it up the hard muscle of his calf. Instead, she picked up her crystal water glass with trembling fingers and took a deep swallow, wondering if it might not be far wiser to douse herself with the icy water.

Drew suddenly gasped and jerked backward so quickly his chair almost toppled over. "What was that?"

For a horrifying instant, Tina wondered if her foot had followed her instincts after all. Then she glanced under the table and, with a sigh of relief, saw that her shoe was still on her foot where it belonged. A further survey caught Aster slinking away.

"It was the cat," she said.

"Which one?" Billy wanted to know, before Tina could shut him up.

"How many do you have?" Drew asked.

"Let's see," Billy began. "There's Jake and Lucifer and Marian and..."

"It was Aster," Tina said quickly, but not quickly enough.

"There are eight altogether," Billy said cheerfully.

"Eight?" Drew gulped, then sneezed. And sneezed again. His eyes started watering.

"Bless you," Sarah and Juliet said in unison.

"Thank you."

"Wait," Billy said. "There are nine now, aren't there, Tina? I'd forgotten about the one that Tiger brought home yesterday."

Drew appeared stunned. "My Lord!"

"Mr. Landry!" Grandmother Sarah protested.

"Sorry, ma'am," he said, and Tina had to restrain a chuckle. She wondered if Drew had been chastised that effectively since he'd left the cradle. Considering the fierce scowls of which he was capable, she doubted it.

"Don't you like cats, Mr. Landry?" Aunt Juliet said. "That could be a bit of a problem. Tina loves them so."

"It's not that I don't like them. I'm allergic to them." He sneezed again, as if to emphasize the point.

Tina briefly considered rounding every one of them up and bringing them into the dining room, but Drew's earlier assessment of her manners kept her from fueling his criticism.

"Billy, get Aster out of here, please," she requested. "And make sure the others are in one of the back rooms or upstairs someplace."

"What about Panther?"

Drew's eyes widened considerably. "You have a panther here?"

"Of course not," Billy said disgustedly. "Panther is a dog."

There was a sudden twinkle in Drew's eyes, and his lips curved into a grin. "Obviously. How foolish of me. I hesitate to ask, but is Panther the only dog?"

Tina shrugged. "He was yesterday. It's hard to say today. Sometimes he brings home friends."

"Naturally," Drew said dryly.

Once the animals had been hidden away, dinner went relatively smoothly. To Grandmother Sarah's smug satisfaction, Drew ate two helpings of everything, including the cherry pie, and exclaimed over the fresh vegetables from Mr. Kelly's garden.

"Compost," Mr. Kelly informed him. "You have to have good compost."

"I'm sure Mr. Landry isn't interested in how you fertilize the garden," Tina interrupted.

"What's that?" Mr. Kelly asked loudly, and Tina realized he'd left his hearing aid upstairs again.

"I said that Mr. Landry probably doesn't care about fertilizer."

"Course he does," Mr. Kelly retorted, scowling at her. "A man can never know too much about fertilizer. How else do you expect him to grow decent vegetables?"

"I'm sure Mr. Landry doesn't grow his own vegetables. He probably has them shipped in seasonally."

"As a matter of fact, I do," Drew said, his gaze challenging hers. Cool blue ice taunting amber fire. "From my farm in Iowa."

Tina's mouth dropped open. "You own a farm?"

"I was born on one. My father still lives there."

"Why, that's wonderful," Grandmother Sarah said, when Tina couldn't seem to think of a single thing to

utter to a man who'd just destroyed every precon-
ceived notion she had about him.

She had figured that Drew Landry had grown up
attending the best schools in Europe, playing squash
or polo with princes and spending his summers on the
Riviera courting beautiful young heiresses. That was
the life-style of most of Palm Beach's winter resi-
dents. From the late 1800s when Henry Morrison
Flagler had built the first railroad into South Florida,
the city had been the resort of the wealthy. Even in the
early days hotel suites at the Royal Poinciana had gone
for one hundred dollars a night at the height of the
season. She'd figured Drew for one of those whose
families had been ensconced here for generations. Instead, he was a farmer. Astonishing!

"I've always thought a man who understands the
earth is much wiser than those fellows who spend all
their time tinkering around with computers and that
kind of nonsense," Sarah continued, ignoring Tina's
increasingly stunned expression. Harrington Industries had been built on the fortunes of the computer
boom, Tina groused mentally. You'd think Sarah
would at least feign approval of the company that kept
food on their table.

"The earth will be here long after all these mechan-
ical gizmos break down," Sarah said, returning Tina's
scowl with a defiant look of her own.

"That's just what my father used to say," Drew
agreed, still staring into Tina's flashing eyes with an
amused, penetrating look that said volumes about
what he was reading in her mind.

Grandmother Sarah obviously caught the flare of sparks arcing between the two, because she hopped out of her chair and began bustling around. "Come on, Juliet, let's clean up these dishes."

"I'll clean up," Tina said. "That's my job."

"Not tonight, dear. You and Mr. Landry go out on the terrace and enjoy the breeze. There's a full moon tonight," Sarah added pointedly.

Juliet sighed and gazed wistfully at Mr. Kelly. "Oh, my, yes. It's very romantic."

Tina tried one last time. "Why don't all of you go on outside then? Billy will help me with the dishes."

Billy groaned, but it didn't matter anyway. She might as well have been talking into the wind for all the attention they paid her as they scurried off to the kitchen carrying plates and glasses.

Drew stood up and offered her his hand, an all-too-enticing gleam in his eyes. "Come on, Mrs. Harrington," he said in a low, provocative voice that sent a flurry of sparks cascading down her spine. "Let's not disappoint them."

Disappoint them? She wanted to strangle them.

Chapter Three

Tina reluctantly led the way out to the terrace, where a strong ocean breeze had swept in at sunset to make the palm trees sway and whisper. The black velvet of the sky was scattered with diamond sparkles. The air smelled of salt spray and the sweetness of tropical flowers. It was a night for romance, which made it about as dangerous for her to be out here alone with Drew Landry as it had been for Adam to be in the Garden of Eden with Eve. She had one edge on Adam, though. She was aware of the potential dangers.

"Let's take a walk," Drew suggested.

"Where?" Tina's immediate caution brought an amused smile to his lips.

"Your tone's not very flattering," he taunted. "You sound as though you think I might be planning to skip the review by HRS and take you straight to the gallows myself.''

Tina was not worried about the gallows. She was concerned about something far worse. In fact, by comparison, the gallows would have been a quick and easy way to go. Spending secluded time with Drew Landry in an atmosphere as ripe for seduction as this one seemed like torture.

"You haven't exactly done a lot to encourage my trust," she responded.

He gazed down at her with his blue eyes. A tanned finger reached over and gently followed the curve of her cheek, leaving behind a path of fire. She was as much startled by the touch's tenderness as by the sensation it aroused.

"Let's see if we can't change all that," he said softly. "Tonight I've discovered that I want very much for you to trust me."

Her breath caught in her throat and she asked in a choked whisper, "Why?"

"Because you intrigue me, Tina Harrington. You're not what I expected at all. You're not like any woman I've ever known. You're like fire and ice, scratchy wool and soft satin, a prickly cactus and a delicate orchid. The contradictions are fascinating."

"Is that your poetic way of saying that after the women who fall all over you, I'm a challenge?"

Her spirited response drew another high-voltage smile. "Perhaps. Couldn't we start over?"

As the promise of his words whispered over her, Tina felt an aching tug deep inside. She couldn't draw her eyes away from his gaze, though she wanted to desperately. She felt as though she were losing her will, as though she were watching her hard-won independence slip away. But when a smile revealed his wicked dimple and he added questioningly, "Deal?" she could only nod and fight the urge to kiss that dimple.

"Then let's start by taking that walk."

Silently, they walked around the house and crossed the narrow road to the beach, where the ocean pounded against the shore with the same wild turbulence that stirred Tina's blood. The wind whipped her hair about her face and teased her flesh in a way that hinted strongly at the effect Drew's deft touches might have. They went down the wooden stairs, and at the bottom, Tina braced herself on the weathered railing, slipping off her shoes before she and Drew set off across the soft, damp sand.

Their way was lit by a spectacular full moon hanging low on the horizon, reminding her once more that it was, indeed, a night made for lovers. And here she was with an attractive, surprisingly charming man who—just as surprisingly—made her blood sizzle.

Despite the pounding of her heart and the responsiveness of her reawakening body, she couldn't forget that the real reason they were together had nothing to do with love or even physical attraction. They had been brought together by his intention to force Sarah, Juliet and the rest out of her house. How could she and Drew start over with that between them?

They began walking hand in hand—she wasn't quite sure how *that* had happened—their silence a counterpoint to the crashing waves. Suddenly, Tina stopped in her tracks, determined to make him see what he was setting out to destroy. Surely there was some compassion in him, some sense of decency that would respond to her pleas. But when she looked up at him, ready to fight for her friends and her way of life, the expression in his eyes captured her and held her silent.

"Tina," he said quietly, her name floating away on a gust of wind just as his mouth came down to meet hers. His mouth was oh-so-soft yet commanding as he took gentle possession, waiting for her to relax into the kiss, persuading her lips to part. His tongue teased against her mouth until her body screamed for him to claim her more intimately. As if he'd read her mind, the moist velvet of his tongue darted inside, taunting her with yet another suggestion of the powerful, shattering intimacies that could rise between them.

From the moment that he'd taken her in his arms, Tina had sensed an inevitability that had shaken her. This man was a danger to her happiness, her serenity. Yet her body had responded to him in a way that spoke of acceptance and yearning and a desire so intense, so all-consuming it was like nothing she had ever known before, not even with Gerald. With Gerald she had felt respected, even loved, but she had never experienced this shattering femininity.

When the kiss ended at last—far too soon, yet not nearly soon enough—only his hands on her arms stilled her trembling. Nothing short of an explosive joining, however, could ease the throbbing ache she felt and she knew it. Dear Lord, how well she knew it! The realization terrified her and made her more skittish than ever.

"I'm sorry," he apologized, then shook his head, unable to keep the sparkle out of his eyes. "No, I'm not. I've wanted to do that from the minute I saw you this afternoon."

He paused thoughtfully. "Come to think of it, I think I even wanted to do it weeks ago, when you came over and stood there valiantly defending Billy in front of my shattered window, then demanded that I return his baseball. I'm fascinated by women with spirit."

The solemnity of his words reached in and captured a tiny part of Tina's heart, but still she was puzzled. "If you felt that way, then why did you stir up all this fuss over the way I live? You had to know it would infuriate me." She tilted her head to study him more closely. "Or were you one of those kids who showed affection by pulling a girl's hair?"

He winced. "I hope my approach has always been much smoother than that. I gave my first love a bouquet of dandelions. We were seven. I've graduated to roses now."

"I'd have settled for dandelions," Tina retorted. "It would have been a whole lot better than a letter from HRS. That was not the best way you could have demonstrated your interest."

"Actually one thing has nothing to do with the other."

"It certainly does. You can't reject part of me and want the rest."

"Oh, can't I?" he said dryly. Then he sighed. "Okay. On a rational level, you're probably right. But I didn't understand before."

"Understand what?"

"What was really going on at your house. The way it was presented to me, it all sounded sinister."

Tina couldn't restrain the grin that spread over her face and lit her eyes. "Like in some gothic novel?"

"Not quite that dark and mysterious, perhaps," he admitted. "Right after I moved in, I got a couple of anonymous letters, a phone call or two. I started asking around, and a few of your other neighbors confirmed that you'd been taking in all these strange people since your husband died, giving them the run of the place. They implied they were worried about you, but now it's evident they were more concerned about what it might do to the neighborhood, if somebody didn't put a stop to it. You're a powerful lady. They weren't willing to risk your wrath. They figured I'd have nothing to lose." His expression turned grim. "I also have something of a reputation for dealing with situations like this."

"So you decided to take my life-style on as your own personal crusade without even talking to me?"

"Well, the evidence did seem to be pretty clear-cut. The people were living here and the zoning laws are very specific about these being single family dwellings, not some sort of glorified rooming houses."

"Except for the servants' quarters, of course," she countered.

He caught the dry note in her voice. "Of course."

"What about the state? Why did you have to drag them into it?"

"You may not believe this, but I was actually concerned about the people you have staying here. I kept thinking how I'd feel if it were my father living in some unlicensed place that nobody'd checked out.''

"What?" Tina couldn't have been more shocked by his unspoken innuendo. It was as if he'd flat-out accused her of being a mass murderer. She missed the odd, faraway look that came into his eyes and shadowed their usual brightness. "That's the most ridiculous thing I've ever heard. Did you think I was holding them prisoner and starving them all to death, for heaven's sakes?"

He had the good grace to look embarrassed. "Well, I had no way of knowing what kind of crazy crank you might be, or whether they were old and rich and senile. Nobody bothered to tell me you were a feisty, sophisticated lady with a quirky sense of humor. They said you were a widow, that you'd been a little odd since your husband's death. For all I knew, you could have been getting senile, as well."

"At my age?"

"They didn't mention your age either, and Gerald, after all, was quite a bit older."

"He wasn't *that* old." She stared innocently up at him. "He was about your age, as a matter of fact."

"Touché."

"Of course, you saw no need to check any of this for yourself? You'd make a terrific journalist," she said sarcastically.

He winced as her shot hit its mark. "I knew that senility wasn't the problem when you came over to defend Billy. Still, you could have been bilking a bunch of sweet old folks for every penny they had. You wouldn't be the first person to do something like that. Some of the best con artists look absolutely harmless, but they prey on the helpless."

"Does Grandmother Sarah strike you as helpless? Or Mr. Kelly?"

"No. Of course not." His eyes sparkled wickedly. "Then, again, there is Aunt Juliet..."

"I am not bilking Aunt Juliet. She doesn't have anything to steal. And don't you kid yourself, she's not as helpless as she may seem. You saw what happened when you tried to cheat at Scrabble."

"I know that now," he said softly. "And I've seen you with those people. I know that you really do love them and that they love you."

"If you'd taken the time to find that out first before going off half-cocked, it could have kept me out of this mess." She stared up at him with eyes that were suddenly tear-filled. She hated showing him even this tiny sign of weakness, but she was angry and frustrated and scared. Her life had been lonely for so long after Gerald died and now, just when she'd found happiness again, it was threatened.

"Now you've gone and ruined everything," she murmured.

He brushed away the single tear that rolled down her cheek. "Come now. There's no real harm done."

"No real harm?" She regarded him disbelievingly. "For one thing, do you have any idea what this kind of publicity could do to Harrington Industries? The board will think I'm off my rocker and try to yank the chairmanship away from me. There are a few of them who've already got a candidate in mind and have been looking for any excuse to push him forward. You've just given them a dandy one."

"They don't know a thing about this. It hasn't been in the papers yet."

Tina regarded him as if he'd lost his mind. "How long do you think it will take for some ambitious reporter to discover that the state thinks I'm operating an unregulated foster home for wayward kids and stray adults?"

"I'll go in tomorrow and withdraw the complaint. That should be the end of it."

"You really did grow up on some piddly little farm in Iowa, didn't you?"

"Actually, it was a pretty big farm. With hundreds of acres of corn," he retorted with that beguiling twinkle back in his eye. Tina glowered at him. He was not making her feel one bit better.

"My point is that you're naive if you believe the state will simply say thanks for telling us about the mistake and go on to something else. They've been under a lot of pressure lately for not being too thorough in the past. I'm a well-known lady. It will be a terrific publicity coup. They can show they weren't afraid to take on a big shot. Just to be safe, they're going to have a whole crew of inspectors crawling all over the place to be sure I'm not a raving lunatic and that the estate meets a zillion dumb sanitation requirements..."

He grinned at her rantings and, despite herself, her anger faded just a bit. "No problem. I'll vouch for your sanity and you must have half a dozen bathrooms in that place," he said encouragingly.

"Ten, actually, but that won't stop them from sending inspectors down here from Tallahassee to count them. What if they make Sarah and Juliet and the rest of them leave? They don't have any place to go."

"Tina, that's not going to happen. I'm sure once you explain it to them, they'll understand. I do."

She gazed at him with renewed hope. If she could convince Drew Landry then maybe she could convince the state. "You do?"

"Well, I'm not exactly sure how they all landed on your doorstep, but I understand that there's nothing illegal about what you're doing. I doubt if you're even violating the zoning code. I'll back you up one hundred percent."

"Thanks. Will that keep me out of jail?" she asked sarcastically.

He patted her arm and, if it hadn't felt so good, she'd have hit him for being so patronizing. "Don't go getting hysterical," he soothed. "Nobody's going to jail."

"I wouldn't be so sure of that if I were you. Palm Beach has some mighty peculiar laws."

"And I'm sure you have some bright lawyers on staff at Harrington Industries. If you don't, I have a few myself, but," he said emphatically, tilting her chin until her gaze met his, "it is not going to come to that. I won't let it."

Tina sighed and wondered exactly when Drew Landry had set himself up as her protector. She wasn't sure she liked him in that role any better than she'd liked him as the enemy. "*You won't let it?* Did they hold an election and name you governor?"

"I may not be governor, but I do have a certain amount of clout."

"And you're planning to rush in and save my hide, a hide which wouldn't be in danger in the first place if you'd kept your nose on your side of the hedge?"

"You don't sound appreciative."

"I prefer to fight my own battles."

"Independence can get pretty lonely."

"Maybe so, but then you have no one to blame but yourself for the outcome."

"Do you object to letting me help at least?"

"I suppose not," she said so reluctantly that it brought yet another grin to his lips.

He drew her to the stairs leading up to the road and pulled her beside him on the bottom step. "If I'm going to help, I need to know everything. Tell me, how did they all come to be living with you? I mean they don't seem to be the kind of people you'd meet at a charity gala or on a cruise on the *QE II.*"

Tina explained about her meeting on the beach with Grandmother Sarah. "We got to talking and one thing led to another and she moved in the next day."

"You invited her home just like that? Without doing a security check?" He sounded horrified. "She could have been an ax murderer."

Tina glowered at him. "Does that sweet little old lady who just baked you a cherry pie strike you as an ax murderer?"

"Well, no." he admitted. "But in your position you can't be too careful."

Tina threw up her hands. "You're pre-judging again. I thought you said you liked my friends now that you've gotten to know them."

"Well, I do, but it's because I've gotten to know them."

"You've talked to them for exactly two hours," she pointed out. "Are your instincts supposed to be better than mine?"

"No, but . . ."

Her eyes flashed dangerously. "If you say anything about your being a man and my being a woman, I will dump sand down your trousers."

"You are a woman," he noted dryly. "As for your threat, it raises some interesting possibilities."

"Never mind."

"Okay, let's forget about our respective abilities to judge character for the moment. Where did you meet up with Mr. Kelly?"

"He was my neighbor when I was growing up. He was always like a surrogate grandfather to me. His wife died a few months ago, and all of his kids have moved away. I couldn't bear the thought of him in that tumbledown old house all by himself. He put up quite a fuss, said he'd lived there all his life and, by golly, he wasn't going to move out now." She mimicked Mr. Kelly's grumpy tone perfectly.

Drew chuckled.

"What's so funny?"

"I was just trying to imagine how you talked him into it."

"Well, it was a rather high-spirited conversation. I started out by telling him to stop being a stubborn old mule, and he told me to quit being an obstinate brat."

"Sounds like you were off to a typically diplomatic start."

"Then I wised up and began telling him how crummy my grounds looked. If there's one thing Mr. Kelly can't stand, it's weeds messing up a perfectly good landscape. When I told him the tomato vines were practically wilting because I didn't know what to do with them, he packed up his tools and moved the next day. He said he was only going to stay till he got things straightened out around here, but that was six months ago. I think he's realized things will never be completely straightened out here and he's terrified Aunt Juliet will start dabbling in his garden."

"What about Aunt Juliet? Where did you find her?"

"Actually she and Billy came together, a few weeks after Sarah. Billy broke into one of the Harrington Industries offices, and the police called me down to the station. I found out that he and his great-aunt were living on her Social Security check in a dump that wasn't fit for the rats who shared with them."

Tina's voice shook with indignation. "You should have seen it. It was a disgrace. The landlord—an even bigger rat—was charging them practically every penny she got from the government. That's why Billy had broken into the office. He was trying to find something he could fence to buy food and medicine for Juliet."

"So, of course, you dropped the charges and brought them home."

She lifted her chin defiantly. "What else was I supposed to do? Leave them there?"

"There are agencies—"

"Which are overburdened as it is. Besides, once you get caught up in that cycle, you never get out." She stared out at the ocean, then said softly, "I saw it happen to too many of my friends when I was growing up. I wasn't going to let it happen to Juliet and Billy."

She regarded Drew hopefully. "Billy's not a bad kid. You can see that, can't you?"

"He did break my window," he reminded her, but his tone was teasing.

"It was a great hit."

Drew chuckled. "It certainly was. Right straight into my kitchen. The cook is still shaking and threatening to quit."

"Is that why you called the authorities? So you could hang on to your cook?"

"I'd starve without her."

"I'm sure Grandmother Sarah would be thrilled to pieces to feed you."

"I'll keep that in mind."

"Will you really withdraw the complaint in the morning?"

"I told you I would."

"I'm coming with you."

"Still don't trust me, huh?" he taunted.

"It's not that. They may have questions that you can't answer."

He shrugged. "If I don't know the answer, I'll make one up."

"Terrific. Then you'll land in the cell next door to mine, charged with perjury."

"We could hold hands through the bars."

Tina's heart skipped a couple of beats. "Nice try, but no dice. I'm going with you."

"I'll pick you up at nine, and we can drive over to West Palm Beach together."

"Maybe Sarah, Juliet and Mr. Kelly ought to come along. They could help explain."

Drew simply stared at her. "Are you crazy?"

"They're rational adults...well, most of them are," she corrected when his brow quirked skeptically. "Anyway, they have a perfect right to live anywhere they like."

"With the possible exception of a Palm Beach estate," Drew noted dryly.

His words, meant in jest, sent a shiver of dread over Tina. He was undoubtedly right. It was better if they remained safely at home. She shivered at the possibility that her household might very well be broken up if she and Drew were unsuccessful in the morning.

"Drew, what am I going to do if they say they can't stay?"

He put an arm around her and pulled her close. For a moment she allowed herself to revel in the sensations that closeness aroused. She felt safe—and threatened—all at the same time. Her body's response was all too disturbing, so she decided to pretend she didn't notice it. After several seconds, she realized that her powers of pretense must have deserted her. The sensations were there, stronger than ever, and the look in Drew's eyes was fueling them.

"You know what I think, Tina Harrington?" he said softly.

"What?" she asked shakily.

"That you're getting as much out of this arrangement as they are."

"Of course I am. I told you that. They're like family to me."

"But why would a lovely young woman like you need to take in strays to have a family? Surely there are men ready to serenade beneath your balcony, court you with lavish gifts, tempt you with romantic trips, fill all of those bedrooms with gorgeous children."

"A few," she agreed. "But that's not enough."

His eyes sparkled back at her wickedly. "It's not? Lord, woman, what do you want?"

She chuckled. "You know what I mean."

"No. Tell me."

"I never know if it's me they want or Harrington Industries," she confessed wistfully.

"I see."

Tina wondered if he did. Even as a teenager of limited financial means, she'd never had a doubt about her attractiveness to boys. She'd known they dated her because they found her pretty, with her shining, wavy hair, wide amber eyes and slender figure, or because they enjoyed her impish humor, or were challenged by her sharp wit. It certainly wasn't because she was rich.

The same had certainly been true when she'd met Gerald. She'd had nothing to offer him but the shrewd business acumen she'd been on the verge of attaining, her gentle manner and all of her love. For him, that had been more than enough.

But now she was worth a small fortune, and it tended to get in the way. When she saw a sparkle in a man's eyes, she was never sure whether it was a reaction to her perfume or the smell of her money.

So she had filled in the empty spaces in her life with people who needed her as a friend, not a wealthy benefactor or stepping-stone to corporate greatness. It also helped her to repay in some small way the wonderful things that had come her way when she had fallen in love with Gerald. It had been too late, by then, to help her parents. She was convinced they had died from struggling too long against life's hard knocks. Once they'd seen her happily settled, they had simply given up the fight, passing away within months of each other.

There were a lot of emotions at war within her these days. Anger at her parents' sad lot in life, gratitude for her own blessings, determination to make what she could of all that Gerald had left her despite the board of directors and a tremendous fear of being used. All but the last had made her strong. The fear had made her cautious.

It was that caution that told her she should run from Drew Landry while she still could. It was the strength that told her she needn't fear him or anyone. Except, perhaps, the HRS.

Settling for détente between her conflicting emotions, she said, "I think we should be getting back," and got to her feet. "They'll be wondering what happened to us."

"Judging from the look in Grandmother Sarah's eyes when we left, she'll be hoping she already knows exactly what happened to us," he replied as they went back to the estate.

Fortunately, it was too dark for him to see the blush that spread up her cheeks. "So you noticed that?"

"How could I miss it? She practically swept us out the door with a broom."

"Don't mind her. She's a bit of a romantic."

"So's Aunt Juliet, it appears. Think there's any chance for her and Mr. Kelly?"

"Not if she tries to put petunias in his vegetable garden. He'll go after her with a trowel, and then we really will be in trouble around here."

They had reached the terrace, and Drew stood looking as though he couldn't quite decide whether to go or stay. Tina wasn't about to help him out.

"I don't suppose you're going to offer me a nightcap?"

"I hadn't planned on it," she teased.

"If I asked for one, would you deny me?"

She shook her head and saw the smile on his lips just before they brushed oh-so-lightly across her own and sent waves of delightful, pulsing heat over her.

"Are you asking?" she said breathlessly.

"Nope," he said, giving her a jaunty wave as he strolled away. "It's no fun if you have to ask. See you in the morning, angel."

"See you," she said softly, her eyes following him until he'd slipped into the shadows and was lost to her view. She wrapped her arms around her middle and hugged, wondering at the strangely empty feeling that suddenly taunted her. The howl of the wind was suddenly lonely rather than exciting. Just a minute ago, she'd felt...what? Alive? Elated? Dangerously provocative?

Dangerous. That was the operative word here. Drew Landry represented danger and excitement and all the things she'd been missing. Until now, she'd had no idea that there was an empty space in her life that Grandmother Sarah and the others couldn't fill. She hadn't realized it until Drew had vanished into the shadows and left her alone again.

She turned around quickly and ran smack into someone who let out a groan at the impact.

"Mr. Kelly, I'm sorry," she apologized, then noted his pajamas and the dazed expression in his eyes. He was sleepwalking again.

"Come on, Mr. Kelly," she said gently, taking him by the hand. "Back to bed with you."

"Damn petunias," he muttered.

"Ssh. I won't let Aunt Juliet put her petunias anywhere near your garden."

He blinked and gave Tina a sharp glance. "What's that, girl? Speak up."

"I said I'd keep Aunt Juliet away from your garden."

"You'd better. That woman's a menace with those frilly little flowers of hers. I'll dig her her own damn garden if she wants one, long as she stays away from mine."

Tina smiled. "I'm sure she'll love that. Now you come on, Mr. Kelly. Let's get you back to bed."

"I can get back to bed perfectly well on my own, young lady." He scowled at her. "And don't you forget it."

Tina sighed as he marched toward the winding staircase, his back as straight as a royal palm and twice as stiff.

"I love you, Mr. Kelly," she murmured after his retreating form.

"So," came an interested female voice from the shadows. Tina couldn't see much, but she recognized that voice and its determined tone. "What did you think?"

"About what, Sarah?" she replied innocently.

"Don't go all vague on me, young lady. About Drew Landry, of course."

"He's interesting." It seemed a safe enough description.

Sarah emerged from her hiding place and smiled smugly. "I knew it. I knew he was perfect for you. Why that man has pizzazz and sex appeal and brains. You'd have to be plum crazy to miss it."

"I only said the man was interesting, for heaven's sakes. I didn't say a thing about his sex appeal."

"It was your tone, dear. There's interesting and then there's *interesting*."

Tina groaned. She'd known this was going to happen. "I am not discussing this," she said, stomping off into the house muttering under her breath.

"Interesting." She tried the word out, once out of earshot, then tried it again. "Interesting. *Interesting*. Oh, hell."

Chapter Four

When Drew rang the doorbell in the morning, the household was in its usual state of chaos. This kept Tina from fully appreciating the knockout effect of Drew in a dark suit, crisp white shirt and pin-striped tie, which was probably just as well. It was disconcerting to discover that he had the same devastating power over her senses at the crack of dawn as he did by moonlight.

"Where's my homework?" Billy shouted from the top of the stairs just as her gaze left the Italian leather shoes, moved up over the blade-sharp crease in Drew's trousers and took in the superb fit of the jacket over his magnificent shoulders. She was on her way back for another dreamy look into Drew's eyes when she was forced to drag her attention from the dressed-for-success man on her doorstep to the disorganized kid upstairs.

Billy and homework were not compatible. It was his firm conviction that it was contrived as a punishment for sins he'd committed in a past life and that he had no obligation to pay for mistakes he didn't remember making. On the rare occasions when he actually did his assignments, he either lost them on the way to school, forgot them, or spilled orange juice all over them. His grades weren't helped one bit.

"Did you do it?" Tina asked, gesturing for Drew to come in. Two of the cats immediately wound themselves affectionately around his ankles, rubbing hair all over the dark suit, while Panther sat eyeing him hopefully. Drew grimaced at the cats, sneezed three times, then gave the dog a distracted pat. All the while his gaze was focused so intensely on Tina that she felt a flush of heat stain her cheeks.

Oblivious to the electricity that crackled in the air in the foyer, Billy scowled down at her, indignation written all over his freckled face. "Of course I did it. It was an essay for English."

In that case, Tina thought, it was probably just as well that he couldn't find it. Billy seemed to have difficulty putting the English language down on paper. Not only was his spelling unrecognizable, he'd picked up a good bit of Lady MacBeth's vocabulary and wasn't above using it on his teacher for shock value.

Sixty-three-year-old Viola Maxwell was not unlike Grandmother Sarah in her ability to convey Southern gentility at its most innocent. She and Tina had had several conversations about Billy's rather unusual and provocative impressions of the world around him. Miss Maxwell seemed to feel that Billy would benefit from a sterner hand—and perhaps several years in a military school environment.

Tina couldn't bring herself to tell Billy to stop doing his English assignments. She'd tried to channel his creative energies in a less controversial direction, but when that hadn't worked, she had, on occasion, hidden the papers. This, however, was not one of those times. She'd been too distracted last night to even go looking for his homework to inspect it.

Billy regarded her all too knowingly. "You didn't hide it somewhere, did you?"

Tina stole a quick look at Drew and noted that he was watching the exchange with interest. She coughed and stared at the chandelier. The crystals needed cleaning. She'd have to remind Mr. Kelly. She didn't want Aunt Juliet climbing any more ladders. The last time, she'd kicked it over and dangled from the chandelier for five minutes before anyone had noticed.

"Why would I steal your homework?" Tina finally muttered, wishing they hadn't had this discussion in front of Drew. He already thought she was slightly, albeit intriguingly, off balance. This might not add much strength to her cause of presenting herself as a rational, intelligent woman.

"So old straitlaced Maxwell wouldn't get embarrassed," Billy said bluntly.

"What exactly did you write about?" Drew inquired, with increased interest. He'd apparently caught the guilty gleam in Tina's eyes. That, combined with Billy's accusation, was enough mystery to rouse the curiosity of a saint, much less a man who was already known to meddle where he wasn't supposed to.

"It was sort of about sex," Billy mumbled.

Tina's brows lifted as Drew choked back a laugh. "Sort of? What exactly was the assignment?" She could not imagine Viola Maxwell assigning that particular subject. In fact, she doubted if the woman was even familiar with it. She seemed a little sheltered.

"She wanted us to write about something we knew."

"And you know about sex?"

"Well, some stuff. You know, the guys talk and all."

Tina decided the conversation had gone on long enough. If she didn't stop it now, Billy might very well enlighten Drew on exactly what the guys talked about. She, for one, didn't want to hear it, especially not in front of a man who had her thinking all too much about sex as it was.

"Billy, I think perhaps you ought to select another topic. You have a study hall this morning, don't you?" she said quickly.

"Yeah, but I was planning to use it to do my math homework."

"Why didn't you do your math last night?"

"Because I was going to do it in study hall."

Tina rolled her eyes. "Use your study hall to write a new essay," she said sternly. "And tonight we're going to have a talk about your schoolwork."

"Oh, Tina, come on," he groaned. "We talk about that all the time."

"That's because we have this problem all the time. Now get on down here for breakfast. Grandmother Sarah is waiting."

Billy ran down the stairs, gave Drew a man-to-man wink and headed straight for the dining room. Drew and Tina exchanged glances.

"Someone needs to have a talk with that boy and not about homework," Drew said, then sneezed again as the cats meowed at his feet.

"Well, I certainly can't do it," Tina grumbled, grabbing the friendly cats and putting them outside. "Maybe if you've had a kid since he was a baby you can tell him about the birds and bees, but I got this one nearly fully grown. Considering where he'd been hanging out when I met him, he probably knows more than I do."

"Want me to talk to him?"

It would mean Drew Landry would have one more toe in the door, but Tina didn't think she was up to fighting him on this one. "That might be a good idea," she agreed readily. "I can't quite see Aunt Juliet or Sarah doing it, and if Mr. Kelly talked to him, he'd probably forget to wear his hearing aid and we'd all hear every word."

"I'll do it," Drew promised as he followed her into the dining room where Mr. Kelly and Aunt Juliet were arguing heatedly about where to put her petunia bed.

"Wouldn't it be nice to have it right by your vegetable garden?" Juliet said, clasping her hands in excitement. "Then we'd be able to chat while we work."

Only an innate gentlemanly politeness kept Mr. Kelly from telling Aunt Juliet what he thought of that idea. Tina could see his gnarled fists clenching under the table, as he shot her an I-told-you-so glare.

"Nope," he growled, shaking his head adamantly. "You don't want 'em there. Too much sun. They'll wilt and die. I'll make a border 'round the gazebo. That's the place for flowers like that. Give it some color and all."

The gazebo did not need color any more than Alaska needed more snow. It had purple bougainvillea climbing all over it. But Tina knew exactly what Mr. Kelly's clever reasoning was. If Aunt Juliet were clear out by the gazebo, not even with his hearing aid would he be able to pick up her running commentary on the weather and what it might do to "her damn frilly flowers."

"I wish one of you would tell me what you want for breakfast," Grandmother Sarah inserted in the middle of the debate. "I'm not hanging around in the kitchen all day long. I have more important things to do."

"Like what?" Mr. Kelly retorted. "You gonna knit some more of those lacy things to put around on the tables so everything will slip right off? It's a wonder there's a lamp left in the place, way those things slide."

"They're crocheted, not knitted," Sarah replied stiffly, her blue eyes flashing. "And things wouldn't slide if some people were more careful."

"I'll have a cup of coffee," Drew said above the din, earning a beaming smile from Sarah. Tina gave him credit for tactful diplomacy. Another two minutes of that familiar debate and Grandmother Sarah would have left the room in a huff. She made the doilies not because she especially liked them, but because she considered crocheting therapy for her arthritic fingers. But she wasn't about to tell Mr. Kelly that, so she just suffered his gibes stoically.

"Thank goodness," Sarah murmured to Drew. "At last someone who knows his own mind. How about some scrambled eggs and toast to go with that?"

"You'd better take it," Tina urged with an impish grin. "Otherwise, you'll end up with oatmeal like the rest of us. That's what she gives us when she's mad."

"I am not mad," Sarah huffed. *"If some people...."*

"Eggs would be great," Drew interrupted, and Sarah bustled out of the room after scowling at Mr. Kelly one more time for good measure.

Then Drew turned his gaze on Tina, who'd dressed in her very best corporate image—navy suit, white linen blouse, navy and white low-heeled pumps and a strand of pearls—for their meeting with the officials at the Department of Health and Rehabilitative Services. He tilted his head and examined her from head to toe, his wicked eyes lingering and caressing as effectively as a lover's touch. She had the distinct impression he'd liked her better in her sundress. In fact, she thought maybe he was stripping her right out of the clothes she had on. It made her heart pound a little faster, which was not the way she wanted to start the day. She wanted to be prepared for those state officials. She didn't want to be so shaken up by Drew Landry that they slipped something past her. She took a deep breath and squared her shoulders.

Suddenly Drew was grinning at her.

"What's so funny?" she grumbled.

"You look as though you're steeling yourself to go to war."

"I am."

"Want to talk strategy?"

She glanced around the table pointedly and shook her head. "Not now. We'll discuss it in the car on the way over."

"Over where?" Aunt Juliet immediately wanted to know. She was quick as a whip when she wanted to be. "Aren't you going to work today, dear?"

"Of course, but Mr. Landry and I have a meeting to go to first."

Aunt Juliet suddenly clapped delightedly, her brown eyes twinkling as though they'd just let her in on an exciting secret. "You're meeting with the minister, aren't you? Oh, Tina dear, that's just wonderful. I do hope you'll let me play the organ."

"The minister?" they both said blankly.

"About your wedding, of course. I'll start today practicing 'Oh Promise Me' or would you rather have something else? I'm sure I could find a lovely ballad."

Tina struggled for composure and absolutely refused to look Drew in the eye. She knew they'd be sparkling with laughter. She reached over and patted Aunt Juliet's hand. "We're not getting married."

"You're not? Did something happen?" Aunt Juliet's expression was so thoroughly woebegone that Tina looked at Drew helplessly.

"What Tina means is that we're not getting married right away," he said, ignoring Tina's gasp of dismay. "We thought it would be better to wait until we know each other a little better."

"I suppose that's wise," Aunt Juliet agreed, then she regarded Drew sternly. "Just don't you go breaking our Tina's heart or you'll have us to answer to. Do you understand me, young man?"

"I would never hurt Tina," he said gently. He gazed directly into Tina's eyes. "I promise."

While Drew ate his scrambled eggs, Tina stirred her oatmeal around in the bowl and wondered just when he'd gotten so sure of himself. He'd kissed her once. They weren't living in the Middle Ages, when that kiss would have been tantamount to a proposal.

She was still wondering about that when they left for the local HRS office in West Palm Beach. The drive seemed to take forever, and Tina was on the edge of her seat all the way. She wasn't sure if she was more nervous about the meeting or Drew's intentions, which were apparently far different today than they had been less than twenty-four hours ago when he'd regarded her as nothing more than a questionable neighbor.

"Are you sure you wouldn't rather let me handle this?" Drew asked again as he pulled into a parking space. "I'm the one who started it."

"I have to be there," Tina insisted, marching briskly up the walk and into the building. "If anything happened and I wasn't there, I'd never be able to forgive myself."

"Or me?"

Tina sighed. "Or you."

"What do you plan to say?"

Tina was already halfway down the hall toward the office of the man who'd sent the official letters. She stopped in her tracks and stared at him.

"I have no idea," she said blankly. She shook her head and started to turn back, muttering, "I'm not ready for this. I've never gone into a meeting without reports and statistics and graphs to prove my point."

Drew squeezed her hand. "You don't need all that stuff for this. Just tell your story. No one could ever doubt your sincerity."

"You did."

"That was before I got to know you."

"And you think this Mr. Grant is going to get to know me in the fifteen minutes he'll probably allot for this meeting?"

"If he's any good at his job, he will." He scanned her face closely. "Ready now?"

Tina managed a tremulous smile, then reminded herself that she'd handled difficult board members and corporate negotiations with aplomb. There was no reason she couldn't deal with one overworked HRS official. "I'm ready," she said firmly.

"Then let's do it."

Once Edward Grant had agreed to see them without an appointment, the meeting started out well enough. Mr. Grant was a tall, thin, bespectacled man in an ill-fitting suit that was just as gray as the few remaining strands of his hair. His smile was harried and his desk was cluttered, giving the impression of a man caught on the brink of chaos.

Tina described each of her houseguests in a way that captured Mr. Grant's full attention. He was chuckling when she finished recounting the morning's battle over the location of the ill-fated petunias. She concluded with a heartfelt little speech about how much having Grandmother Sarah and the others in her home meant to her.

"They're my family," she said simply, as Drew nodded in agreement.

"It's true, Mr. Grant. I've had a chance to spend some time with them recently, and it's a wonderful thing Mrs. Harrington is doing for these people. They would be out on the street or wards of the state if it weren't for her generosity and affection. She's not taking advantage of them, as I first feared."

Edward Grant sighed heavily. "It's true that the state has more than enough cases to deal with," he acknowledged, shuffling through a huge pile of folders on his desk in search of Tina's. When he found it, he flipped it open to Drew's letter and scanned the contents. He peered over the top of his glasses at Drew, his expression puzzled.

"But I have your letter right here, and you did seem very certain that there was a problem. These are serious allegations. Didn't you check into them before making them, Mr. Landry?"

Drew and Tina exchanged glances. His expression was every bit as guilty as it should have been. "I'd been informed about what was going on by some individuals who obviously did not have complete information," he admitted. "Unfortunately, because of my own emotional reaction to situations like this, I'm afraid I reacted without checking out the facts. I take full responsibility for the mistake."

"And now you're satisfied that there's no problem?"

"Absolutely."

"Certainly I trust your judgment, Mr. Landry. I've done some checking. You have an excellent reputation, as does Mrs. Harrington. Still, we can't be too careful. We can't risk overlooking something. You wouldn't believe how many times we visit our clients, check to see that their living conditions are adequate, only to find later that something was amiss. We can't afford to have another black mark against our reputation. The media..." His voice trailed off and he shook his head. "Well, you both know how things can get distorted, and with a case like this, they would have a field day."

"But Mrs. Harrington is hardly operating a traditional state-regulated facility. She simply has a few friends visiting for an extended period of time," Drew argued, as Tina stifled the urge to chuckle at his blatant theft of her own words.

Edward Grant tapped the folder on his desk and stared at the ceiling. Tina guessed he was torn between getting one more case off of his obviously overcrowded desk and doing a tedious, time-consuming investigation. His brow puckered with a little frown and finally he pursed his lips and gazed at her sternly.

"You do understand that we can't have unlicensed facilities operating in this state. We have a large elderly population and we must protect their rights against unscrupulous people."

"Of course. I'm not operating such a facility. These people truly are my friends. I would never exploit them in any way. If a prominent family invited friends to spend the winter at their home a few miles away, you wouldn't question that, would you?"

Mr. Grant looked startled just as she'd anticipated he would. "Of course not!"

"This is virtually the same thing." She didn't point out that her friends were staying a little longer than the typical houseguest. As far as she could see, it shouldn't even be relevant.

"And you agree with what Mrs. Harrington is saying, Mr. Landry?"

"Absolutely."

He smiled, and Tina thought she also heard a sigh of relief. "Then perhaps we could put the case on hold for the time being."

"That would be wonderful," Tina said. "I promise you my guests will be well taken care of."

"If we get another complaint, though, I will have to take action," he said sternly. "The penalties can be quite severe."

Before he could go on, Aunt Juliet, Grandmother Sarah and Mr. Kelly came barging in, ignoring the protests of the harried receptionist. Tina stared at them with a horrified expression. Drew groaned.

"What are you doing here?" Tina gasped, hoping by some miracle she could make them vanish.

"We came to help, dear," Grandmother Sarah said. "We found that letter and just put two and two together and figured out where you and Mr. Landry must be."

"That's right," Mr. Kelly agreed and gave Mr. Grant a fierce scowl. "Can't go putting a woman in jail for what she's done."

"Nobody's going to put Tina in jail, Mr. Kelly," Drew soothed.

"What's that?"

"I said nobody's going to jail," Drew shouted, then muttered, "Oh, to hell with it."

Aunt Juliet was clinging to Mr. Kelly's arm and staring around with frightened eyes. "I don't like this place," she announced.

Tina stood up and went to her, putting an arm around her plump shoulders. "You don't have to stay here, Aunt Juliet. You can all go back home now. Everything has been taken care of."

"Wait a minute," Mr. Grant said. "As long as these folks are here, we might as well hear from them. Have a seat ladies, sir."

When chairs had been drawn up and everyone was seated, he leaned back and said, "Well, now, why don't you all tell me a bit about where you live. You all reside with Mrs. Harrington, is that right?"

"Yes, indeed," Sarah replied, her hands folded primly in her lap. "She took me in off the streets...or rather the beach. I don't know what I would have done if she hadn't come along. They were about to tear down the rooming house where I'd been living, and on my income you can't find too much, just a room with a hot plate most times. I never dreamed I could live in a house like Tina's."

"And do you pay her?"

Sarah looked wary.

"Well, do you?" Mr. Grant persisted.

"Not exactly."

"What do you do...exactly?"

Sarah scowled at him. "I give her my Social Security check every month, if that's what you mean."

"Why do you do that?"

"Why to pay for things, of course. None of us takes charity, young man. We all do what we can. Mr. Kelly does a lot of work around there. I don't know how he manages everything. You should see our vegetables. We should have brought you some. The green beans are especially good now." She beamed at Mr. Grant then and added brightly, "And he keeps the grounds absolutely beautiful. Why there's not a golf course in town that has prettier, greener grass."

"Well, don't give me too much credit now, Sarah," Mr. Kelly said. "You do a bang-up job in the kitchen, and Juliet here, she works around that house like a regular white tornado. There's not a speck of dust in the place."

"And does Mrs. Harrington pay you for taking such good care of her home?" Mr. Grant inquired with a decided edge to his voice. Tina did not like the sound of his tone or his frown. In fact, she had a feeling the direction of this meeting had just taken a sharp turn toward trouble.

"Of course not," they said in chorus.

"Let me get this straight then. You turn all of your money over to her and take care of her home, but she doesn't pay you a dime?"

"Oh, my God," Tina mumbled and rolled her eyes heavenward.

"I don't know what you're implying about Tina, young man," Grandmother Sarah said, "but I don't like the sound of it."

"I'm not implying anything. You've just admitted that this woman is ripping you off."

Tina groaned and three pairs of eyes widened in dismay as the allegation sank in. Sarah was the first to recover and her eyes flashed.

"Fiddlesticks!" she exclaimed angrily. "That is not what we said, young man, and don't you go trying to put words in our mouths. Tina doesn't have a mean bone in her body. She certainly isn't capable of ripping us off. She's like a daughter to all of us. Except Billy, of course. She's more like a mother to him." She turned her blue eyes on Drew and pleaded, "Mr. Landry, do something."

"It's okay, Sarah," he soothed. "We'll straighten this out. Mr. Grant just misunderstood." He got to his feet and leaned over the desk until he was practically nose-to-nose with Edward Grant. "Didn't you?"

"I understand perfectly," Mr. Grant said defiantly. "I will be over tomorrow morning at eight to check into this further."

Ignoring their protests, he ushered them out the door, clucking his tongue disapprovingly. Tina felt more like a criminal than ever.

Next the five of them stood in the foyer of the building, their voices raised in a babble of questions until Tina felt like screaming. Why had Sarah, Juliet and Mr. Kelly come storming in there just when she and Drew had everything under control? True, she'd initially thought having them with her might be a good idea, but she had decided their words would get all twisted around. Drew had certainly realized it.

Now what? They had only wanted to help. She knew that. But now they were in worse shape than ever.

"Okay, everyone, calm down," she said at last.

"Tina dear, we're so sorry," Grandmother Sarah said. "Everything really is a mess now, isn't it?"

"It will be okay. You go on home. I'll think of something."

"We'll think of something," Drew corrected. Sarah and Juliet beamed at him as though he possessed some magic wand and had offered to wave it around in their behalf. It irritated the daylights out of Tina that they were relying on Drew rather than her. Why did everyone always just assume that a man could solve anything? Especially this particular man?

"What's that?" Mr. Kelly asked.

"We're going to take care of everything," Drew said more loudly. "Go on home now. Tina and I will discuss this and come up with a plan."

But as Drew drove the shaken Tina to Harrington Industries, they were both silent. Not even the clear, sparkling sky or wind-whipped water cheered her as it usually did as they drove along curving Flagler Drive. She didn't have a single idea about how to go about convincing the state that she wasn't ripping off her friends, taking their scanty resources to pad her already extensive bank balance. The whole thing was absurd, and yet Edward Grant had taken the facts and twisted them into what he apparently considered a believable con artist's scheme.

During her childhood, Tina had seen many of her elderly neighbors affected by such unscrupulous individuals. She could understand Mr. Grant's transformation from friendliness to chilly distrust. Clearly, he too had seen all too many situations in which the elderly were abused, either financially, psychologically or both. How could she make him see that there was a difference, that their household was filled with a protective warmth and love? Would he be able to tell, as Drew had, simply by walking through the door?

And it had come to this because of a few anonymous letters and Drew's uninformed actions. She scowled over at him.

"I want you at my house at eight o'clock."

He grinned. "Great. We can talk afterward. What's Grandmother Sarah fixing for dinner tonight?"

"No dinner. No talking. I meant in the morning."

"Why?"

"Because when those inspectors start counting bathrooms and interviewing my friends, I want you to watch."

"To make sure they don't say or do anything crazy again?" he said.

"No. So you can see my world falling apart."

"Maybe we should go for coffee and talk about this now," Drew suggested. "You seem upset."

"Upset? I'm more than upset," she retorted, her eyes flashing. "In fact, if I weren't trying very hard to be a lady, I'd tell you in no uncertain terms exactly what I think of you and your meddling.''

"I think you've made your point anyway," he said dryly.

"Good."

Not only was she furious and frustrated by a bureaucracy that allowed no room for human compassion, she was also mad as hell because the man who'd stirred up this hornet's nest still made her pulse race.

Then again, maybe your pulse was supposed to race when you were contemplating murder.

When she got out of Drew's car, she glowered at him and slammed the door so hard that the sports car that could hug a curve at ninety miles an hour bounced on its expensive racing tires. Drew flinched, but she had a feeling he was smiling as she stalked away. She also thought she heard him murmur something about spunk.

Damn the man! Before this was over, she'd show him the real meaning of the word.

Chapter Five

The swift, silent ride to the penthouse of the Harrington Industries tower in West Palm Beach did nothing to soothe Tina's fury, despite the spectacular view she had from the glass elevator of the inland waterway and the pastel Palm Beach skyline. Normally that view, shimmering in the soft morning sunlight like a Monet painting, took her breath away, but today she was hardly even aware of it.

She was still seething as she marched down the hall to her office, her back ramrod straight. The language she was muttering under her breath would have appalled Grandmother Sarah.

Outside the double mahogany doors on which her name was displayed on a discreet brass plaque, she paused and took a deep breath. Determined not to carry her rotten mood through those doors, she plastered a cheerful smile on her face. It lasted approximately fifteen seconds.

"Thank God," Jennifer Kramer breathed when Tina walked in. Normally cool and self-possessed, with twenty-five years' experience as an executive secretary, Jennifer right now looked wild-eyed. Tina didn't have to ask why.

All six phone lines were ringing at once. There was already a stack of pink message slips on the corner of Jennifer's desk including, Tina noted as she flipped through them, two inquiries from reporters, thereby proving once again that it didn't take long for bad news to get around. Her encounter with HRS just might have set a speed record, though.

As if that weren't bad enough, one of the company's directors was pacing the outer office, a cigar clamped between his teeth and a fierce scowl on his face. The place reeked of foul-smelling smoke, indicating he'd been there quite a while.

Tina took one look at what was going on. She tore up the messages, put the calls on hold, ordered her frazzled secretary to take a coffee break and glowered at Mr. John J. Parsons III until his face turned from beet red to a more normal skin tone. Then she waved him into her office, gestured to a chair and took the call on the first line.

She twirled her swivel chair away from Mr. Parsons to gaze out the window at the water as she talked. She rather wished she were on one of the majestic sailboats skimming past. She didn't even much care where it was headed as long as it was away from the irritatingly sexy Drew Landry and the problems he'd brought down on her head at the worst possible time.

"Yes, Mr. Davis," she said politely to the caller's loudspoken inquiry about his minimal dividend check. The man owned a hundred shares of stock and behaved as though he held the controlling interest in the company. He always demanded to speak to her. Most of the time she could deal with him, but today he was sorely testing what remained of her patience. She was absolutely astonished that her tone was actually civil.

"No, Mr. Davis," she said. "I'm sure it will all be straightened out. I'll have my assistant check into it right away. Thank you so much for calling, Mr. Davis. It was good to talk to you."

It took every bit of will power in her to keep from adding, "Go to hell, Mr. Davis." Only an image of Grandmother Sarah's horror and Gerald's disapproval kept her from doing it.

Gerald had believed that every stockholder, as well as every customer, deserved courtesy and prompt, reliable service. It was why Harrington Industries had survived the softening of the computer market. There were incredible, well-publicized stories of the lengths to which Harrington Industries would go to satisfy its customers, including the time Gerald had flown with an entire system halfway across the country and installed it himself to meet a deadline. Tina was not about to ruin that reputation by snapping back at a man whose calls to her were probably the highlight of his lonely day. She made a note to have David check into Mr. Davis's problem and get back to him.

She managed to be equally pleasant to Kathryn Sawyer, who had the personality of a barracuda and a more substantial five percent of Harrington Industries' stock. Tina was going to need that five percent if her ouster came to a vote at the stockholder's meeting at the end of the month. They had even moved the annual meeting to New York to accommodate Kathryn the Great, as she was referred to in the society pages. She was hosting a charity gala there the night after the meeting and couldn't possibly get away, her secretary had huffily informed Tina.

Thanks to Gerald, Tina held more stock than any other single stockholder, but if they all teamed up against her in a coup attempt, Kathryn Sawyer could provide the swing votes Tina needed to remain in power. Tina would have moved the meeting to the middle of the Sahara, if Kathryn had wanted it there. Kathryn, unfortunately, knew it.

"Tina, these next few weeks are critical," Kathryn warned unnecessarily. No one knew that better than Tina. "I've already been approached by some individuals from the board about whether I'd support a change at the top."

Tina sucked in her breath. "And what did you say?"

"I said I was withholding judgment, but for the moment I was inclined to continue backing you. Don't make me regret that."

"Kathryn, I assure you that I'm doing everything in my power to keep things running smoothly," she said, rubbing her temples. A dull throb had started in her head.

The thought of being ousted as head of Harrington Industries had kept Tina awake nights for months now. Although she was the only official nominee for chairman, this was not the first time she'd heard of the rumblings that she was too inexperienced to hold the job. She feared if this HRS business got out of hand, the rumblings could turn into a roar. Even before this had started, she had worriedly prowled the grounds of the estate at three in the morning almost as frequently as Mr. Kelly. She, however, was awake, though sometimes she wished she weren't.

When she'd first been promoted to the position of Gerald's executive assistant years earlier, there had been rumors that she'd only moved up by sleeping with the boss. Many of his senior officers had resented what they considered to be her unearned access to the company's chief executive officer. When she and Gerald had married, the stories had gotten increasingly vicious.

No one stopped to take into account how hard she worked. No one considered how much Gerald loved his company. He would never have risked its wellbeing by putting someone incapable in charge. Tina was inexperienced, but she'd been a fast learner. It was true that she'd had to replace Gerald far too soon, but she understood his vision and she knew how to carry it out. The bottom line reflected that, but there were still those who could be swayed by her lack of experience or innuendos about her capabilities. The bottom line might not matter to those individuals whose actions were tied to emotions, rather than business sense. She could be replaced.

Tina sighed wearily as she listened only partially to Kathryn Sawyer. She had to resolve this mess Drew Landry had gotten her into before it blew up in the press. Then she could count on the company's annual report to speak for itself and her future at the helm of Harrington Industries would be assured, just as Gerald had wanted.

And just as she deserved! That vindication meant a lot to the insecure girl that still lurked inside the successful woman. Oh, she had enough faith in herself to believe that she could work her way to the top again at some other company, but Harrington Industries had been Gerald's legacy. For that reason alone, she had to succeed.

When she'd heard all of Kathryn Sawyer's monologue and promised her that the luncheon planned for the stockholders would indeed be a suitably elegant feast, she hung up the phone and turned reluctantly to Mr. Parsons, whose cigar smoke was making her sick to her stomach.

"What can I do for you?" she asked, giving him her full attention and shoving an ashtray in his direction. He ignored it and tapped the cigar distractedly. Ashes fell to her lovely sea-green carpeting. Tina winced, but kept smiling even though she feared her complexion would soon match the color of the carpet.

"I've been hearing things, young lady."

Tina blanched. Please, God, not already. "What things, Mr. Parsons?" she asked cautiously.

"Talk is we're getting into something new, something downright un-American."

Tina closed her eyes and counted to ten, decided she needed to count to a hundred if she was to hear this conversation out and turned back toward the window. It could have been worse, she reminded herself. He could know about Sarah and the others. When she turned back at last, she asked calmly, "Mr. Parsons, I'm not aware of anything like that. Could you be more specific?"

"Germs, Mrs. Harrington. Germs."

Tina had to choke back a sudden desire to chuckle. She gulped and said, "Germs, Mr. Parsons? I don't understand."

"I hear we're selling germs to those bloody Commies. Now you tell me, is that something a fine company like this ought to be doing?"

"Absolutely not, Mr. Parsons," she agreed wholeheartedly.

He eyed her warily. "Then there's no truth to it? You're sure about that?"

"I am absolutely certain about it. We're still in the computer business. There's not a germ in the place."

He nodded in satisfaction. "That's good, Mrs. Harrington. I must say I'm relieved." He hefted himself out of his chair and waved his cigar at her. "I'll be on my way now. Have to get to the club in time for lunch. Keep up the good work."

Fortunately he was gone before she had to manage another comment. She wasn't sure she could have gotten a single word past the laughter that was bubbling up. She was roaring when Jennifer peeked in the door, her eyes bright with curiosity.

"Are you okay?" she asked hesitantly.

Tina laughed even harder until tears were streaming down her cheeks. She tried to answer and couldn't. She gestured for her secretary to come in.

"What was that all about?" Jennifer asked as she came in waving a can of lilac-scented air spray that was reserved entirely for Mr. Parsons's all-too-frequent visits.

"He was afraid we were climbing into bed with the Commies."

Jennifer blinked and stared. "Are you dating someone I need to run a security check on?"

"Hardly," Tina retorted, then thought of Drew. She wondered what a security check of him would reveal. She really knew very little about the man except what Sarah had read in the gossip columns and the occasional items she'd seen in the *Wall Street Journal*.

Drew Landry had a reputation for gobbling up failing companies and turning them into moneymakers. The possibility that he might be viewing Harrington Industries as an acquisition flitted through her mind and just as quickly was put to rest. The company was not failing, and Drew had never even mentioned Harrington Industries to her. He'd only been interested in her personal life.

Jennifer sat down in the chair Mr. Parsons had vacated, shot a spray of air freshener in Tina's direction and demanded, "Hey, wake up. Explain about the Commies, please. I have grandchildren to think about."

"If I understood Mr. Parsons correctly, he was afraid we were about to sell a formula for germicidal warfare to foreign agents."

"Is that what Tim is working on in that lab?" Jennifer asked, wide-eyed.

Tina glowered at her. "Don't be cute."

"Well, you never know with an inventor."

"Our inventors still deal in computers."

"Thank God. I need this job."

"You'll keep it if you'll get me a strawberry milk shake and two aspirins in the next five minutes."

"Coming right up," she said, bustling from the room. "By the way, those reports you wanted on the new laser chip are on your desk."

"Thanks, Jen."

When the fifty-year-old woman, who'd been an enormous help to Tina in the months following Gerald's death, had gone, Tina picked up the reports, stared at them blindly and put them right back down. An image of Drew as he climbed from his pool and stared at her boldly flashed through her mind. It was an image that stirred an unsettling ache of need deep in her abdomen. After a lifetime of caution, of planning and struggling, Drew made her want to take risks.

She hadn't reacted that way to a man either before or after Gerald. He had been her first love, and the magic between them had been so sweetly satisfying that she hadn't looked at another man since his death. Not even Martin, though they'd been dating for months now.

She remembered the day she and Gerald had met as clearly as if it had been yesterday. She was already working in the Harrington Industries management training program. He'd sent for her one day, only a few months after she'd joined the firm. She'd gotten off the elevator with her knees shaking, feeling exactly like a terrified school kid who'd been ordered to the principal's office. She'd sat in his outer office, oblivious to Jennifer's smiles of encouragement, and tried to imagine what awful thing she'd done and whether it had been bad enough to get her fired.

Instead, Gerald had praised her report. He thought it showed initiative as well as an astute understanding of the computer industry's future. They had discussed it for hours, until finally he'd realized that it was past dinnertime. He'd invited her to join him for a late supper. It turned out to be the first of many such long, quiet evenings during which he built her confidence and taught her everything he knew.

When it evolved into something more, Tina had thought she'd been granted the world. It had been a rude awakening to discover that not everyone was equally thrilled with her good fortune, but Gerald had given her the strength to ignore their jealous insinuations.

"Are you happy with me?" he'd asked.

"Blissfully."

"Then what do they matter?" he'd always said, then kissed her and caressed her until her doubts were banished by his gentle loving.

Tina sighed when she heard the tap on the door. So much joy and so little time to share it, but she'd never forget. When the tap came again, she forced aside the past and returned to the present.

"Come on in, Jennifer."

Her secretary slipped through the narrowest possible opening, then shut the door behind her, her expression dazed.

"There is an absolute hunk outside and he insists that you two have an appointment," she said in a hushed voice.

"Do we?"

"There are no hunks on your calendar, but if I were you, I'd ask him in anyway."

Tina grinned. Jennifer was notoriously interested in her social life—or lack of one. "Does this hunk have a name?"

"Drew Landry."

"I should have known," Tina mumbled.

"What?"

"Never mind."

"Shall I send him in?"

"Why not? He's already ruined my morning. I might as well give him a shot at my afternoon."

The door creaked open. "I heard that and I take exception," Drew said, marching in with Tina's milk shake container and her aspirin. He grinned at Jennifer. "Thanks for pleading my case."

"Anytime. If she turns you down, I'm free for lunch."

Drew's smile widened as he gazed at Tina. "Are you going to turn me down?"

"You haven't asked me anything yet."

"True. I want you to play hooky and spend the afternoon with me."

"That didn't sound like a question."

"Actually it was more in the nature of an order. You've been working much too hard."

Tina's brows lifted quizzically as Jennifer openly listened, her eyes sparkling with interest.

"You've known me less than twenty-four hours," Tina reminded him. "How would you know how hard I work?"

"Grandmother Sarah told me when I stopped by your house."

"When did you do that?"

"After I dropped you off. She says you never get home before eight anymore. You don't get enough exercise, and she thinks you're looking peaked."

"She always thinks I look peaked just because I do not sit out in the sun and blister my skin to a disgusting shade of pink," Tina grumbled. "I'm healthy as an ox."

"Well, you do have circles under your eyes," Jennifer offered. "Maybe you are coming down with something."

"Thanks a lot." Tina was not going to explain that the man standing there looking as though he'd just returned from a week at a seaside health spa was responsible for any circles she might have.

"So, are you coming? I promise you it will be more fun than this watery milk shake, a couple of aspirin and a bunch of dreary paperwork."

She tilted her chin. "Have you forgotten that I'm mad at you?"

"How could I? If you'd slammed the door of my car any harder, it would probably have had a concussion."

"I don't think cars have concussions."

"Have you ever talked to an engine? They're very sensitive."

Tina moaned and buried her head in her arms. She peeked up at him. "You're not one of those, are you?"

"One of those what?"

"Those people who think their cars are human."

"My car is human," he said indignantly. "And we've had a long and very rewarding relationship. I expect you'll grow to love her too, once you've taken a few hairpin curves in her."

Tina shuddered. "I don't do hairpin curves."

"So we'll stay on the expressway today. Are you coming or not? Time's wasting." He leaned across her desk, just as he had Edward Grant's earlier. Tina doubted if the caseworker's heart had thudded quite the way hers was.

"Go," Jennifer urged. "I'll cancel your appointments. Besides, if you stay here, you'll have to deal with all those reporters."

"Reporters?" Drew lifted his eyebrows.

"News gets around fast," Tina said succinctly. Drew had no trouble interpreting her meaning.

"I'm sorry, Tina. I really thought we could keep this quiet."

Jennifer's eyes lit up. "You mean you two—"

"No," Tina practically shouted before Jennifer could join in Aunt Juliet's fantasy. "It's a long story." She looked at Drew, thought about the reporters, and nodded. It was definitely the lesser of two evils. "I'll go."

Once they were in Drew's sleek automobile, she regarded him curiously. The man continued to amaze her. A few days ago he'd been ready to try to convict her for abusing the elderly. Now he seemed to have set himself up as a member of the family. "Why did you stop by the house?"

"I wanted to be sure everyone had calmed down."

"Had they?"

"No. They were still very upset by what happened at HRS this morning. They felt as though they'd let you down."

"Let me down? How? By telling the truth? It's not their fault that Edward Grant managed to turn the truth into something ugly."

"That's what I told them."

"Did they buy it?"

"I'm not sure. Grandmother Sarah was crocheting like mad when I left, if that's any indication."

"It is. It means she's worried sick."

"I was afraid of that."

"How about Juliet and Mr. Kelly?"

"Mr. Kelly was up to his elbows in dirt and petunias with Juliet supervising."

"That ought to keep them distracted for a while then. I'll talk to them tonight."

Drew glanced away from the road and met her gaze. His smile was tender and filled with concern. "They're tougher than you think, Tina. They'll be just fine."

"I know that. It's just that I hate to see them worry. I thought living with me would end their worries."

"A little worrying makes you grateful for what you have."

"I'll remind you of that little bit of armchair philosophy the next time you try to drag me out of my office just to distract me from my problems."

"Ahh, but you're a different case."

"Oh, really? How so?"

"You have me to protect you from things. I could probably even give you some advice on Harrington Industries, if you wanted it. It would make Grandmother Sarah very happy if someone took some of that load off of your shoulders. She thinks you're too young to be buried under paperwork. She also thinks you're more worried than you're letting on about the stockholders' meeting."

"My shoulders are doing just fine. Did someone appoint you as my dragon slayer or did you volunteer for the role?" Tina said with an edge to her voice that Drew apparently missed.

"Grandmother Sarah hinted, but I volunteered," he said lightly. "Gladly."

"Then I hope you won't feel too bad when I fire you."

"You can't fire a dragon slayer," he countered.

"Watch me," she said tightly. "I've told you before that I like to fight my own battles."

"And I like to look out for people I care about," he said just as stubbornly.

"Then I'd say we have a definite problem, don't we?"

"Not the way I see it."

"Oh?"

"I'll just have to make very sure to maintain a low profile, sort of like one of those bodyguards who are meant to be invisible."

Tina suddenly relaxed and laughed. "Drew Landry, you couldn't stay quietly behind the scenes if you tried."

"We'll just have to see about that, won't we?" he said, staring straight at the road. Tina still caught the twinkle in his eyes and knew that the battle was far from over. Drew was a very determined man, who most likely always got what he went after. If he made up his mind that he was going to slay a few dragons for her, she had an awful feeling there wouldn't be much she could do about it. She decided to change the subject instead.

"When are you planning to talk to Billy?"

"I already have."

She regarded him with astonishment. "When on earth did you have time for that?"

"I stopped by his school after I left the house. I was just in time for his study hall."

Tina sighed in exasperation. "Drew, it could have waited. He was supposed to use that study hall to do his English assignment."

"Judging from the conversation you two had this morning, that assignment was best left undone."

The thought of Drew explaining the facts of life to Billy sent a tingling awareness scampering over her flesh. "So, umm, what exactly did you two talk about?"

"Oh, love and sex and stuff," he said, mimicking Billy. "He seemed to think he had the sex part down pretty good."

Tina's eyes widened. "Did he?"

"Let's just say that for his age he had a better than average understanding of the mechanics of it."

"Oh, my God. Has he ... ?"

"I don't think so," Drew said with a definitely wicked sparkle in his eyes. "I decided to concentrate on the emotions in the hope that he might stop and think before he does. The boy is only thirteen, after all."

"Do you think he got the message?"

"Well, judging from his reaction, I think he's going to be keeping a close eye on you and me."

Tina had an awful sinking feeling in the pit of her stomach. "What is that supposed to mean?"

"Well, I sort of used us for comparative purposes."

"You what!"

"Come on, Tina. You have to admit that you and I are attracted to each other. More than attracted, in fact."

"I do not have to admit any such thing," she said, despite a traitorous racing of her pulse.

"You will, if you're honest."

"Humph!"

"At any rate, my point was that you and I are not hopping in the sack just because of a mutual attraction."

"You told a thirteen-year-old boy who lives in my house that? Are you crazy?"

Drew feigned hurt. "I thought I was setting a good example. When you and I go to bed, it will be because of the way we feel about each other."

"When you and I go to bed, there will have to be an ice storm in hell," she snapped.

"Will you feel better if I tell you that it worked? Billy understood exactly what I meant."

"He did?"

"I'd say offhand that he now expects to see a marriage license before he gets the first clue that you and I are sharing more than a chaste kiss good-night. Otherwise, I'm likely to be hammered over the head with his baseball bat," Drew said ruefully. "Talk about protective. That kid has the instincts of a mother hen."

Laughter bubbled forth. "I love it," Tina said. "You built the trap, and it snared you."

He glowered at her. "You don't have to enjoy it quite so much. You're going to wind up just as frustrated as I am."

"Wanna bet?" she retorted. Before she could discover who was actually likely to have the last laugh, she decided she'd better retreat to a safer topic. "How do you manage to have all this free time on your hands to run around and offer advice and consolation? Don't you have a company to run?"

There was a wicked gleam in Drew's eyes as he answered. He obviously saw straight through her ploy. "Yes, but technically I'm on vacation. I've left some very good people in charge of things. They call when they need me, and I touch base a couple of times a day."

"What if they need you while we're out gallivanting?"

"Oh, I think they can spare me for an afternoon. Besides, we are not gallivanting. This trip is business, too."

"Terrific! You're taking me along to a business meeting."

"Not exactly."

"Then where are we going?"

"You'll see."

"Am I dressed properly?"

"If you were dressed any more properly, you could teach in a convent."

"That's not what I meant."

"Let's just say, if you don't think what you're wearing is suitable, you can always take it off."

"Drew!"

His low chuckle sent a wave of heat scampering straight down her abdomen. The memory of her rotten morning fled, and the fact that he never did answer her question sent her imagination soaring in all sorts of wicked and thoroughly inappropriate directions.

She moaned softly as she realized what was happening. It hadn't been ten minutes since Drew had dared her to remain immune to his charms and already she was succumbing. Infuriatingly enough, frustration was apparently not very far away after all.

Chapter Six

With Drew flirting outrageously during the ninety-minute drive to Miami, Tina's traitorous mind explored a whole assortment of interesting possibilities for the afternoon. Although she breathed an outward sigh of relief, she realized she was almost disappointed when he turned into the palm-lined driveway at Hialeah Park. As lovely as the place was, with its lagoons and flamingos and lush tropical plants, it was not a secluded setting for a lovers' rendezvous. There were already thousands of people yelling their heads off as a pack of gleaming Thoroughbreds turned into the homestretch.

"We're going to the races?" she asked thoroughly baffled and trying not to reveal her disappointment. It would make Drew too smug. "I thought you said this was business."

"Actually there's a little stand here that sells great pizza," Drew retorted innocently. "I thought we'd have lunch before I get to work."

She shook her head. "Nobody goes to a racetrack for lunch. You're nuts."

"That's why I fit in so well at your place. Now stop wasting time and let's get moving. I'm starved."

She stared at him. "You really did come here for lunch?"

He shrugged, his grin sending Tina's heart slamming against her ribs again. "Well, I suppose we could watch the races, as long as we're here."

"Gee, what a novel idea!"

Tina had never been closer to the races than her television screen and then only for the Triple Crown events, which Gerald had watched avidly. As soon as Drew had grabbed a couple of slices of pizza, they found seats and within moments Tina found herself fascinated by the spectacle around them. She insisted that Drew explain every bit of the *Racing Form* to her. He pointed out the horses' breeding, the rundown of top trainers, the owners, the current listing of winning jockeys, the speed ratings and the past-performance listings for each horse. She listened intently to every word, asked several questions, then nodded in satisfaction when she'd heard his answers.

"Got it," she said, reaching into her purse and extracting a pocket calculator.

"What are you doing?"

"It all seems pretty scientific. I'll just work out a quick formula based on past performance and speed rating and I should be able to calculate the winners," she said confidently, punching numbers into the calculator for the horses in the third race. She pointedly ignored Drew's expression of amused tolerance.

Oblivious to the smudges of newsprint on her fingers, she concentrated on what she was doing until, ten minutes later, she looked up and announced, "I'm betting on number seven."

"That horse hasn't won a race in the last year," Drew argued. "Don't waste your money."

"But he had one of those dots beside his last workout. You said that was important. And the number-two jockey is riding him. The top jockey isn't even in the race," she countered, airily waving off his obvious intention to argue further.

"Besides," she said with finality, "I saw him when he came on the track and I liked the color of the jockey's shirt. That shade of emerald green is one of my favorites."

"So much for scientific analysis. How much are you wagering on this sure thing?"

"I'll bet two dollars to show," she said decisively and handed him the money.

Drew's lips twitched. "It's nice to see that you have the courage of your convictions."

Tina scowled at him. "Which horse are you betting on, Mr. Know-it-all?"

"I think I'll sit this race out."

"Coward."

"A smart bettor picks his races carefully. He does not bother with a race when the favorite is a sure thing and has such low odds, he'll barely get his money back."

"Forget the favorite. I'm telling you, you should put some money on this horse of mine."

"Tina, the odds are forty-five to one. That horse will be lucky to come in by the end of the afternoon."

"Oh, go place the bet," she muttered in disgust.

Fifteen minutes later she was cashing in her ticket. The horse had cruised across the finish line three lengths ahead of the favorite.

"Don't gloat," Drew growled. "It was beginner's luck."

Tina ignored him. She was already punching numbers into her calculator again.

It wasn't until the ninth race, when her throat was already practically raw from screaming and her pocketbook stuffed with crumpled dollar bills, that she discovered Drew owned a horse running in the day's feature race. Somehow she'd forgotten all about his claim that he had come to the track for business. This was the last thing she'd expected.

Listening to the enthusiastic comments from the crowd around them, she discovered that his stable was reputedly one of the best in the country. Drew's Serendipity Sal was going in as the favorite.

"And I thought you were just a staid old business-man. How did you get into this?" Tina asked as they walked to the paddock area for the saddling. She'd reluctantly put her calculator away. She couldn't very well bet against Drew, anyway.

"I grew up riding," he said, a reflective expression on his face for just an instant. Clearly he was back in Iowa, reliving a time of which Tina knew far too little.

"I've always loved horses," he went on. "But there's something about a Thoroughbred that is almost mystical. These magnificent creatures go faster than the wind. If I weren't so big, I think I'd like to be a jockey. What a thrill it must be to skim over the ground, feeling the muscles of the horse stretch to the limit and knowing that your slightest touch is in control of all that energy."

Tina's eyes were wide and lit with amber fire. "You make it sound incredible."

He regarded her with astonishment. "Haven't you ever ridden?"

"Never. The only horse I've been on was on a merry-go-round in an amusement park."

"I'll take you riding someday, and you'll see for yourself. It won't be the same as this, but it will give you some idea."

"I'd like that." She regarded him quizzically. "I'm still not sure how you wound up as an owner. Did you just go out one day and buy a racehorse?"

Drew chuckled. "It wasn't quite that simple. With the amount of money involved, you don't go into this lightly. I found a trainer who agreed to work with me. As soon as the rest of my business was financially sound, we went to the sales and bought my first racehorse, a two-year-old colt."

His eyes were filled with distant nostalgia. "He was only mediocre on the track, but was he spectacular to watch. After that, I was hooked. I knew, though, that I had to either make a commitment to go with it all the way or drop out. I wouldn't have been satisfied to run a one-horse stable."

His enthusiasm was infectious. "Obviously you went with it. Is your obsession costing you a bundle, or did it turn out to be a good decision?"

He nodded sheepishly. "Actually, it's turned out pretty well."

"How well?"

"I have a farm in central Florida for breeding and training and I have about twenty horses on the track now. This little beauty you're about to see cost $750,000 as a yearling. She's only a four-year-old and she's already won over a million. If she wins today, we'll probably retire her and breed her."

Tina was used to talking big money, but not when it came to something that seemed to her as risky and frivolous as horse racing. When she'd been growing up, her parents had scraped by. She still wasn't used to treating money casually. She shopped in the chain department stores, not the elegant boutiques, and on Sunday mornings both she and Sarah clipped food coupons from the paper.

Now, though, what had always seemed to her to be merely a rich man's hobby took on a whole new meaning. Grandmother Sarah's crocheting and Aunt Juliet's petunias were hobbies. This was big business.

She took a good long look at Serendipity Sal with her gleaming coat and prancing step.

"Nice horse," she commented wryly.

"Are you referring to her looks or her value?"

"I'm impressed by both."

"Just wait until you see her run. That's what it's all about."

As they went back to their box to wait for the start of the mile-and-a-quarter race, Tina's heart pounded in anticipation. Drew trained his binoculars on the starting gate when the gun went off, and when Sal broke badly, Tina could see tiny white lines edge his mouth. But the four-year-old's speed more than made up for the faulty start. By the time the horses reached the backstretch, Sal was running third and gaining.

As they rounded the turn, Sal moved into a neck and neck race with the leader. Tina was jumping up and down, clinging to Drew's arm, her throat parched and scratchy and beyond sound, even though she tried like crazy to yell. When the two horses burst across the finish line in a cloud of red dust, she had no idea which had won.

Frustrated, she caught the amused laughter in Drew's eyes.

"What's so funny?"

"You."

"Oh?"

"For a lady who knew virtually nothing about racing a couple of hours ago, you're hooked, too, aren't you?"

"It's wonderful," she enthused. "One question, though."

"What?"

"Did she win?"

"It's a photo finish. They'll announce it in a minute."

"You mean we have to wait?"

He tapped her on the nose. "Your impatience is showing, Mrs. Harrington."

Tina grimaced. "I know. Patience is not one of my virtues. Ask Grandmother Sarah."

"She did mention that it might be nice if I could slow you down a bit. Haven't you ever had to wait for something? Anticipation is part of the excitement."

"I waited for things most of my life," she replied, suddenly serious. "Now that I can make things happen, waiting makes me crazy."

Drew touched a hand to her cheek, flooding her with warmth. "I can understand that," he said gently, "but don't get so caught up in the action that you forget to stop along the way."

"And smell the roses?" she retorted with a touch of irony.

"Or savor the special moments," he said solemnly, his blue eyes capturing hers, holding her until the world vanished and it was just the two of them, alone in a timeless, reckless place all their own. Tina searched Drew's eyes and found them clear, honest and filled with warmth. The thundering of her heart resounded in her ears, and her lips parted on a soft sigh. Drew lowered his head. His mouth was only a heart-stopping hair's breadth away from hers when an explosion of sound split the air and shattered the moment.

The posting of the results had drawn the crowd to its feet. When she saw that Serendipity Sal was officially in first place, Tina impulsively threw her arms around Drew's neck and kissed him soundly, though without the sweet tension of the kiss they'd lost.

Blue eyes glittered at her dangerously. "You do that again, Tina Harrington, and I won't be responsible for my actions," he warned in a low growl. "We'll never get down to the winner's circle."

"Racing is a sport of gentlemen," she reminded him tartly.

"Actually it was the sport of kings and not all of them were gentlemen. Besides, all sorts of mavericks are into it now," he teased right back, and a tingle of anticipation danced down her spine. Anticipation. She was beginning to see what he meant.

"Like you?"

"Exactly like me."

"Have I mentioned what an enigma you are?"

Drew seemed puzzled. "In what way?"

"If I'd had to describe your personality a day or two ago, I'd have said you were a pompous, meddling, stuffed shirt with the mental diversity of a rabbit."

"How flattering." He actually grinned at her description. "And now?"

"Your mind darts in so many directions, I have trouble keeping up with you. You're filled with contradictions. On the one hand, you strike me as a man who has quite a knack with the ladies. You always know just what to say. Jennifer practically fell at your feet. You've charmed Grandmother Sarah and won Aunt Juliet's heart. On the other hand, you've convinced Mr. Kelly you're the only man in Palm Beach besides him who knows a thing about compost. You're equally at home either here, in a boardroom, or playing Scrabble."

"What about you? Have I won you over yet?"

"With all those other ladies vying for your attention, why does it matter?"

"All those other ladies, hmm? Does the competition bother you?"

"Why should it?" she retorted promptly.

He bent down and brushed a tantalizing kiss across her lips, lingering just long enough for another shock of awareness to rip through her and set her pulse to racing.

"Because you and I are going to have something very special," he said softly, his eyes locked with hers. Tina's breath caught in her throat. "If I were you, I wouldn't want any other woman interfering."

Tina blinked and tore her gaze from his. She managed a shaky laugh. "What arrogance!"

"Actually, I thought I was just being very straightforward. Someday you'll understand that it's a trait I value above all others."

After the ceremony in the winner's circle, they made a brief visit to the barn to see that Serendipity Sal had returned from the race in good condition. She'd been washed and brushed until her chestnut coat was shining in the late afternoon sun. A groom was walking her up and down in front of Drew's stalls.

While Drew chatted with his trainer, Tina leaned against a railing and took a deep breath. An earthy, pungent odor filled the air. It was not at all unpleasant as Mr. Parsons's cigar smoke had been. This was real. She'd never been on a farm, but imagined that this must be what it was like. She tried to envision Drew's home in Iowa and couldn't. Even there, his growing-up would have been so much easier than hers. From what he'd said, it had not been a hand-to-mouth existence as hers had been, or even as so many small farmers lived, their fortunes fluctuating on the success or failure of a single crop, on a fluke of the weather.

She was still thinking that over when they stopped for dinner at a small Cajun restaurant. Once they'd both ordered the spicy, mouth-watering blackened grouper, she sat back with her glass of wine and studied the man across from her. He'd left his jacket in the car and the collar of his shirt was open, revealing a provocative shadowing of dark hairs at the base of his tanned throat.

"What were you like when you were a little boy?" she asked, suddenly feeling a need to go back to a time when Drew would have been less formidable, less boldly masculine. Even now that she'd discovered that his temper flared only under provocation, she still found him to be a bit intimidating. That feeling could merely be from his power over her senses, but it was very real.

"I was a little hellion," he admitted, that faraway look back in his eyes. "I started climbing practically before I could walk, and my dad was constantly having to pull me down from trees, the hayloft, the kitchen counters. No place was safe from my excursions."

"You miss your home, don't you?"

"Sometimes. Life was certainly less complex when I was growing up."

"Was it fun living on a farm?"

"It was incredible. Even on a farm as large as ours, it's not an easy life. You learn responsibility at an early age." He grinned at the memories. "You can't imag-

ine what it was like in the winter, though, when the
snow could block all the roads and we would sit
around the fire and read or watch a movie or TV and
pop popcorn in the fireplace. In the summer I went
skinny-dipping in the stream or rode my horse. As
much as I love it down here, I still miss watching the
change of seasons.''

"We have a change of seasons," Tina countered
with all the defensiveness of a native.

"Sure. The temperature drops ten degrees."

"You sound like a typical northerner. Just because
we don't get snow, doesn't mean we can't tell when
winter comes. All you have to do is go out to the
Everglades and see which birds are here or look at the
flowers that bloom only in the cooler weather."

Her expression went all soft and dreamy. "And then
there are the strawberries." She practically licked her
lips at the thought.

"Strawberries? What do they have to do with winter?"

"You've never gone strawberry picking down here?
What kind of a farmer are you? There's nothing better to do on a winter afternoon than go to a field and
pick fresh strawberries."

"Why don't you just buy them in the store?"

Tina looked scandalized. "It wouldn't be the same
at all. We'll go one day and you'll see. Have I convinced you we have a change of seasons yet?"

"I'm starting to be a believer, especially since there's
also the mosquito test," Drew teased.

"The mosquito test?"

"Sure. If you don't have mosquitoes, then it must be winter."

"I suppose you were never bitten by a mosquito up north?"

"Maybe once or twice," he admitted. "But it was a fluke."

"A fluke, my eye."

"Okay, so we're at a standoff on mosquitoes."

"How did you wind up in Florida? Landry Enterprises is headquartered in Cedar Rapids."

"I first came to Florida because of the horses. Then a friend told me about the house, and I decided to check into it. I thought it might be nice for my father to have someplace to go during the cold weather. At his age the harsh Iowa winters get to him."

"Is he here now?"

"No, but he's due any day. He couldn't seem to make up his mind whether to fly or drive. I suppose I'll hear from him tomorrow or the next day. He's not exactly predictable," he said with fondness in his wry tone that intrigued her.

"Will you only be here through the season then?" she asked, surprised at her sense of disappointment. She'd hoped he might be settling in, that he would be a real neighbor. Maybe even more? No. She wouldn't allow herself to start thinking like that.

"I'll come and go," he said, reaching over to rub his fingers across the knuckles of her clenched fist. "I seem to be discovering a lot of reasons to stay lately."

Tina shivered and met his gaze boldly. "I'm glad," she admitted softly, contradicting her head, which was shouting that she'd only be safe from these disturbing sensations once he was back in Iowa.

"Enough about me now," he said. "I gather you're a Florida native."

"Yep. I was born in West Palm Beach, went to the local junior college and then finished at the University of Florida," she said, watching him for any subtle sign of surprise that she hadn't had a classier background. It didn't seem to faze him at all. "That doesn't bother you?"

He stared at her in astonishment. "Why should it?"

"It bothers a lot of people in Palm Beach and at Harrington Industries. Unless your pedigree is a mile long and your degree is from Harvard, you don't count for much. I mean, where else would the mayor's race involve a descendant of Charlemagne and King Louis XIV running against a descendant of Russian czars?"

"By those standards, I'm just as nouveau riche as you are. The world is full of snobs, Tina. I'm not one of them. I thought we established that last night." He regarded her closely. "Gerald Harrington wasn't a snob, either, was he?"

"No," she said quietly. Unexpected tears suddenly shimmered in her eyes. Sometimes it hit her like a blow that Gerald was truly gone. "Gerald wasn't a snob. He loved everyone. I think that's what made him such an anomaly in the business world. He didn't have a ruthless, unkind bone in his body and yet he succeeded."

"Are you still in love with him?"

Tina sensed the tension as he asked the potentially volatile question and sighed. "I suppose I'll always be in love with him. He was a wonderful man, and I owe him a great deal. He turned my life into a fairy tale. There were times when I felt exactly like Cinderella. I think that's why I want so badly to help Sarah and the others. I was extraordinarily fortunate. I don't ever want to forget that."

"I'm not sure you answered my question. Are you over your husband and ready to go on?"

"Gerald is dead, Drew. I'd be a fool if I clung to the past rather than live in the present."

The tightness around his mouth eased. "I'm glad, Tina." He reached across the table and lifted her hand to his lips. The velvet warmth spread through her, stealing into all the hidden places that had grown so cold since Gerald's fatal accident.

"Tina, maybe it's too soon for me to be saying this, but I have to. I don't want there to be any misunderstandings between us about what I want."

She gave him a puzzled glance, though her heart was skittering crazily. "I don't understand," she said, not meaning the remark to be coy. She needed to have him make his intentions very clear.

"I said it earlier. I want you. I've wanted to make love to you ever since I first laid eyes on you. I don't intend to give up until you want the same thing."

Tina gulped. That was certainly clear enough. Now that he'd said it so plainly, she needed time to absorb it. A lifetime or two ought to do it, but he wasn't going to allow her nearly that long. She tried to look away, but Drew's fingers captured her chin and forced her to meet this gaze. "Could I talk you into coming home with me tonight?"

"You probably could," Tina admitted softly, surprised to find that she was enjoying the purely feminine thrill of watching the heat of desire blaze to life in his eyes. "But I hope you won't try."

"Oh."

She smiled tremulously. "I didn't say never, just not yet, Drew. I don't think either one of us can be sure of our feelings and I know there are too many complications in my life right now."

"And you blame me for at least one of them."

"I don't really blame you, though I still don't understand entirely why you felt you had to meddle in my life-style."

The blue of his eyes darkened. There was so much pain shadowing those eyes that Tina felt the hurt deep inside herself.

"Someday I'll explain it to you," he promised, "but right now I'm more interested in why you won't go home with me when you've admitted that you want to."

"You must read the *Wall Street Journal*. You know that I'm facing a critical board meeting in a few weeks. I have to focus all of my energies on that and on getting HRS off my back. I need some time to put things back on track before I face any sort of personal involvement."

"Am I a distraction, then?" he asked, a teasing glint in his eyes.

"That's one way of putting it."

"Is that your only reason?"

"No," she admitted candidly.

"I didn't think so. What's the rest?"

"Well, from what you said earlier, Billy would heartily disapprove of things heating up so rapidly between the two of us. After your speech on honor and respect and emotional commitment, he'd probably come after you with a shotgun."

"He probably would at that."

Tina didn't add that she also needed some time to sort out her feelings about becoming involved with a man as driven and domineering as Drew Landry, a man capable of wresting control of her life away from her. Although Drew had been supportive so far, she knew that he was also a very protective man. He'd hinted earlier at a willingness to take over Harrington Industries rather than have her worry herself to death over it. It seemed nothing more than honest concern for her well-being, but perhaps it was more.

Tina had learned from experience that too many men saw her as a shortcut to control of Harrington Industries. Things were happening too quickly between her and Drew for her to trust her feelings—or his stated ones—completely. Although she was aggressive and decisive in her business dealings, it was only today that she'd learned to gamble at all. She was not ready to bet with abandon on something as potentially hurtful as a commitment to a man she hardly knew. It would take time for Drew to convince her that his motives were entirely personal and altruistic.

Right now the look in his eyes was certainly personal. It was bold and assessing and heated with desire.

"You take as long as you like to get things back on track, Tina," he said slowly, his voice filled with lazy sensuality. "Just make sure that track leads right next door."

Tina discovered that she wanted desperately to believe he meant what he said, that he would be there when she was ready to take a chance on the future.

Chapter Seven

When Drew turned off the coastal highway into
Tina's driveway, it was close to midnight. His head-
lights picked up Billy's forlorn, hunched figure sitting in the shadows. Lady MacBeth sat on his
shoulder. For once, the normally talkative bird was
absolutely silent. A flutter of dread rippled through
Tina.

Anxious words tumbled out almost incoherently as
she leapt from the car and ran up the walk. "Billy,
what are you doing out here at this hour? Has something happened? Is somebody sick? Are you okay?"

"Sure," he mumbled, swiping at the tears on his
cheeks. He didn't look at her.

Drew approached more slowly and touched a re-
straining hand to Tina's arm. When she would have
probed further, he shook his head, then asked Billy

casually, "Mind if we sit here with you for a while, then? It's a nice night."

Billy shrugged, his gaze still directed toward the ground. They sat down on either side of him, waiting for more, letting the silence go on and on, thickening with an unbearable tension.

"Where is everyone else?" Tina asked finally when she could keep her voice calm.

"Out back, I guess. Maybe they've gone to bed. I don't know."

"Were you waiting for us?"

Suddenly Billy turned to face her, his eyes no longer sad but filled with anger. He drew back a hand as though he wanted to hit her, but at the last second he stopped himself and demanded in a choked whisper, "Why didn't you tell me what was going on? How could you keep something this important from me? Don't I count around here?"

"Tell you what, son?" Drew said when Tina couldn't think of a thing to say in the face of such smoldering rage and heartrending anguish.

"That me and Aunt Juliet are going to have to go away."

"That's not so," Tina said. She reached out to Billy, but he jerked back as though he couldn't bear her touch. His rejection wrenched her heart. From the moment she'd rescued Billy and his aunt, he'd been her adoring shadow. He'd trusted her and now he obviously felt she'd not only betrayed him but was abandoning him as well.

"Billy, no one is going to make you go away. I swear to you, everything is going to work out."

He glowered at her, his eyes disbelieving. "But you didn't tell me anything, and that's not what they were saying tonight. They said some guy's coming in the morning and he's going to make us leave. It'll be just like it was before, when my folks went off and dumped me with Aunt Juliet. We won't have any money, nothing to eat. Aunt Juliet can't live like that. She gets so cold. Last winter she coughed all the time. She should have gone to the doctor, but we didn't have any money."

Billy shuddered, and Tina could only imagine what his memories must be like. He was far too young and vulnerable to have shouldered such responsibilities. She should have seen what the HRS threat would do to him and prepared him for it.

"I promise you, we're going to work this out."

"Why are they coming after all this time? It doesn't make any sense. We've been here for ages."

"It's because of me," Drew admitted. Tina could hear the guilt and sadness in his voice. He was seeing firsthand the traumatic effect of his well-meaning actions. "I filed a complaint."

Billy stared at him in stunned disbelief, his lower lip quivering. "But I thought you liked us. I mean after that talk we had and all, I even thought you and I were going to be pals. Is it because I broke your window? Are you still mad about that?"

"Of course not." Drew swore gently, briefly touching Billy's arm. Tina noticed that the boy didn't pull away from the tender, comforting gesture. "I'm only human, Billy. I made a mistake. A big one. I thought things were different than they are. The people at HRS are making the same mistake. Once they arrive, they'll know better, just like I did."

Billy's gaze swept anxiously over Tina's face. "Do you believe that?"

She embraced him. Though he didn't respond, this time he didn't move away, and her breath escaped in a tiny sigh of relief.

"I have to believe it, Billy. I don't know what I'd do if they ever took you away. You're part of my family now." She managed a tremulous smile for him and brushed the hair off his face. "Now why don't you go on up to bed. Tomorrow's an important day and we all need to be ready for it."

"Can I stay home from school?"

"I don't know. We'll talk about it in the morning."

His lip curled defiantly. "You can't make me go. I want to be here with you."

"We'll talk about it in the morning," she repeated firmly.

Billy's skinny arms wound around her and held her tight. "Don't worry, Tina. I'll tell 'em that we love you. Then they'll have to let us stay, won't they?"

"That might do it," she said, but she wondered if it would be nearly enough.

When Billy had gone inside, Drew pulled Tina into his arms. The tension eased, then fell away as she buried her face in his shoulder, the smooth fabric of his shirt soft against her cheek. His arms were so much stronger than Billy's and just as loving. She let her eyes drift shut. She felt so safe right now, but how long would that fragile feeling last? Would it survive even another twenty-four hours?

"We're only postponing things between us," Drew reminded her as though he'd read her mind. "You and I are going to have our time together someday. This won't change that."

"I hope you're right," she said wistfully, suddenly aware of just how much she needed him in her life. It was too soon to describe that emotion as love, but there was an undeniable aching desire building inside that went straight to her soul.

"I know I'm right, and it's going to be soon, because I'm not sure how long I can wait to hold you in my arms."

She gave him a faltering half smile. "You are holding me in your arms. Should I be insulted that you haven't noticed?"

"I noticed all right, but I'm trying not to think about it." His voice was rough with frustration.

"That doesn't make a lot of sense."

"It does, when you're not sure if you can control yourself."

Tina fiddled flirtatiously with his loosened tie and gazed up at him provocatively through half-lowered lashes. "I thought Drew Landry was the sort of man who was always in control."

Uttering a low groan deep in his throat, Drew stilled her roaming fingers, which were headed daringly down his chest. "He was until he met a bewitching, spirited neighbor, who seems to invite everyone to live with her except him. It's doing terrible things for his ego."

"You have a perfectly good home of your own," she retorted.

He brightened. "If that's what it takes, I'll sell it first thing in the morning."

"Nice try, but I think I'm in enough trouble with the group I've got now."

He sighed heavily, but she noted that the corners of his lips were twitching with amusement. "Okay," he said regretfully. "I guess I'll see you tomorrow."

"You are going to be here when they come, then?"

"Of course. You ordered me to be here."

"And you listened?" she said in mock astonishment. "Amazing. I'll have to remember the technique."

He kissed her lightly. "Don't let it go to your head."

Then he kissed her again, his tongue sliding over velvet softness as ripples of excitement danced along her spine. Her fingers tangled in his dark hair as she held him close, reveling in his strength and his gentleness. Problems that had seemed insurmountable vanished, caught up in a whirlwind of thrilling sensations. She hadn't wanted to feel that way in his arms, hadn't wanted to face the rush of heat and alluring tension that his touch created, but it was there, beyond her control.

Despite her intentions to the contrary, that kiss would have lasted until dawn if Tina had had her way. It would be accompanied by every nuance of lovemaking that she and Drew could explore. Part of her wanted, needed, that tonight, but once again she rejected it as coming at the wrong time. She was attracted to Drew, but she didn't know him. Loving intimacy deserved much more. It deserved a depth of feeling built on trust and sharing, things that couldn't happen overnight.

Breathless, she pulled away as far as Drew's tight embrace would allow. "I think you'd better go."

"Give me a rain check?" he asked and pressed a burning kiss at the hollow in her throat. Flesh that had been cool to the touch turned feverish, and her pulse pounded with a shattering violence. Too much, she thought with a moan. She withdrew from the heated temptation.

"You've got it," she said softly, trailing her fingers along his cheek, astonished at the possessiveness that flared inside her.

And then, just when she would have kept him with her, he was gone and the long, lonely night was all that waited for her.

It was a particularly somber group that gathered to await the arrival of the HRS inspectors. Aunt Juliet was in her usual black attire, which did nothing to brighten the mood. In her nervousness she'd drawn her hair back so tightly that her face had a pinched look.

After much heated discussion about the impression it might make on HRS, Billy had been allowed to stay home from school. Drew's vote had been the clincher. Before Billy came downstairs, he warned them that leaving Billy out would devastate him, shattering the feeling of belonging he'd finally found. The others finally agreed.

Normally, a day off from school would have thrilled Billy. Today, though, he sat next to his aunt, clutching her hand and trying valiantly not to let his own anxiety show.

"I don't suppose anyone wants breakfast," Sarah asked hopefully, twisting her lace-edged hankie with nervous fingers. Not even Drew responded.

"I'll go fix some coffee anyway. We might as well be wide awake for this." She bustled off to the kitchen.

"I can't stand this waiting around," Mr. Kelly grumbled to no one in particular. He stood up and hitched up his khaki pants. "I'm going out to pick tomatoes. Can't let 'em die on the vines just 'cause some fancy bureaucrats take it into their heads to come nosin' around where they don't belong. Anyone wants me that's where I'll be." He stomped off through the French doors. Tina could hear him muttering long after he'd disappeared from sight.

Drew, who'd arrived practically at first light, took Tina's icy hand and held it until she could feel her blood stirring to life. She smiled at him gratefully.

"Are you okay?" he asked, his voice filled with concern.

She nodded. "I'll be fine once this morning is over with. It's the waiting that's killing me. I couldn't sleep last night. Mr. Kelly and I were bumping into each other in the halls all night long."

"Let me handle things," Drew suggested again. "They may listen to me. You're all too emotionally involved."

Tina scowled at him. "Drew, you got us into this."

"Which means it's up to me to get you out."

"You already had a chance yesterday, and it didn't work. Besides, I've told you before that I don't need a protector. I'm perfectly capable of fighting my own battles." She grinned as his jaw set stubbornly. "Drew Landry, I mean it. It's my battle."

"Then what the hell am I doing here if you don't need me?"

"You're here to watch," she reminded him lightly, then sighed and gently touched his cheek. "And I do need you just to be my friend."

"Always," he promised, "but I can't swear I'll be able to keep my mouth shut."

Sarah returned with a silver coffee service just then, but before she could even pour the first cup the doorbell rang. Edward Grant and two young assistants were on the doorstep, all of them carrying battered, bulky briefcases. The introductions were perfunctory. Mr. Grant obviously was as anxious to get through the ordeal as Tina was.

Tina had no sooner escorted them to the living room, than the doorbell rang again. She opened the door this time to find several reporters outside. Most were society-page writers in search of titillating gossip, but a prominent business columnist from Miami was among them, and the sight of him made Tina's blood run cold.

Before she could get the door closed, a dashing, elderly man with a shock of white hair and startlingly familiar blue eyes walked in, followed by the reporters.

"I'm Seth Landry," he told Tina, looking a little bemused by all the confusion. "That son of mine around here someplace? I told him I'd be coming down for a little visit, and he's disappeared. That tight-lipped old butler next door seemed to think he might be here.''

"Of all days," Tina muttered, but she smiled brightly and waved Drew's father vaguely in the direction of the living room where everyone else had gathered. She considered boarding up that awful room with all the combatants inside and then fleeing to Bermuda. It was a very attractive, if cowardly notion. Instead, she took a deep breath and jumped into the fray.

The noise level was so high, it was impossible for Tina to hear herself think. Only Mr. Kelly, returning from the garden and brushing dirt off his trousers, seemed unduly complacent. Tina knew perfectly well that was because his hearing aid was upstairs on his dresser. She almost wished she had one too, so she could shut out the din.

Apparently Mr. Grant was equally dismayed by the unexpected interest in his inspection. He beckoned Tina over.

"I wasn't aware that this would attract quite so much attention," he muttered, blinking at her from behind his glasses. He didn't look nearly as sure of himself as he had yesterday. "Could we go somewhere else to talk?"

"Certainly." She started to lead the way to a cheerful room across the hall, but everyone jumped up to follow them. Mr. Grant, his eyes wide, stared at Tina helplessly. She stifled a grin and said, "Everyone, please. If you'll wait here until I conclude my meeting with the gentlemen from HRS, I'll be happy to answer any questions."

Grumbling, the reporters sat back down. Grandmother Sarah, delighted at finding a way to keep occupied, offered them coffee and fresh-baked blueberry muffins. She recruited Juliet to help.

Billy and Drew, however, were not about to let Tina go off alone with the enemy. "It's okay," she told them.

"Tina, please," Billy pleaded, running his fingers through his slicked-down hair. The gesture created rows of little spikes all over his head. He looked as though he'd stuck a finger in a light socket. "I gotta tell him how I feel."

"You'll get a chance to talk with us, young man," Edward Grant promised, smiling for the first time. That smile, as tepid as it was, gave Tina renewed hope. Billy looked at her and, when she nodded, he retreated to help in the kitchen.

Drew was less easily persuaded. Finally, Tina suggested he stay with Mr. Kelly. "I know he's more upset than he's letting on. It can't be good for his blood pressure. Please, Drew."

"Are you positive you don't need me? I'm sure Dad would be happy to keep Mr. Kelly occupied. They could go out and look at the garden. Dad's crazy about compost."

"Stay with them. I need to do this myself."

"Damn it all, woman," he muttered, but he went.

Tina took Mr. Grant and his assistants through the house. None of them said a word as they saw the rooms in which her friends were staying, each of them bright and cheerful and filled with personal memorabilia. Each also had a private bath. If the inspectors were surprised that Grandmother Sarah and the rest hadn't been banished to servants' quarters or worse, they kept it to themselves. At subtle signals from Mr. Grant, the assistants made frantic notes on forms they carried with them on clipboards.

Back downstairs, Mr. Grant asked if there was someplace where he could interview each of the guests privately. Tina showed him into a room and brought Grandmother Sarah to him. Mr. Kelly followed, and Mr. Grant agreed to interview Billy and Aunt Juliet together at the end.

Tina sat outside the door while the first interview went on and on, her hands folded in her lap. She knew that she appeared totally relaxed. She'd conditioned herself from childhood not to show her emotions and thus upset her parents. It was an ability that had been extraordinarily helpful when she'd been confronted with difficult board members as well. Never once had they been able to read her intentions or her fears.

Despite the outward appearance of calm, the inside of her stomach was churning. When Grandmother Sarah came out, the older woman's expression had brightened considerably. She sat beside Tina and patted her hand.

"Well, now, that wasn't half as bad as I'd expected. Stop fretting. Edward is really quite a nice young man."

"Edward?" Tina glanced at her sharply. "Are you referring to that emotionless automaton inside by his first name?"

"Really, Tina, I'm surprised at you," Sarah scolded. "You're normally quite a good judge of character. Edward is just trying to do his job."

"It's a lousy job," she retorted crossly. "And that's not what you were saying about him yesterday."

"That may be, but I can admit a mistake when I make one. He explained it all very carefully. He has to learn the truth. Not everyone is as lucky as we are."

"Do you think he can see that?"

"I think he'd be a fool if he didn't, and Edward is no fool. Trust me," she said and patted Tina's hand again. "Why don't I send Drew out here to keep you company?"

"I'm not sure I'm speaking to him today after all."

"Oh, posh-tosh. This will be over soon and you'll forget all about it. Don't throw away a chance at an exciting new life over a little thing like this."

"*A little thing?* You think turning our lives upside down is a *little thing*?"

"Come now, Tina. Don't go losing your perspective. I think life gets utterly boring if there's not some sort of disturbance now and again to spark things up."

"*Spark things up,* for heaven's sakes? Just tell me one good thing to come out of all this."

"Why that's easy, child. Just look how much closer we all are now that we see we might lose each other. We appreciate things we'd been taking for granted."

Tina regarded her doubtfully. "I suppose, but I could have appreciated all of you just fine without going to this extreme."

"Maybe. Maybe not," Sarah replied, then gave her a calculated glance. "Then, of course, there's you and Drew."

"No, there's not," Tina insisted stubbornly.

Sarah said with absolute aplomb, "We'll just have to wait and see about that, won't we? I think maybe I'll send him on over to keep you company anyway. He seems to distract you better than I do."

"Humph."

When Drew entered the hallway a few minutes later, he gave her his most dazzling grin. It warmed her down to her toes in spite of her best intentions to keep him at arm's length. If she was going to wind up hating Drew for splitting up her family, she didn't want to have a taste of falling in love with him first.

"Sarah sent me out to cheer you up."

"Actually, I think she'd prefer it if you'd seduce me. She seems to be feeling particularly romantic and philosophical today."

"I'd be happy to oblige with the seduction, if you think HRS wouldn't object to our using one of the bedrooms. I'm afraid we'd draw too big a crowd down here."

Tina suddenly found herself giggling at the thought of all those society writers peeking through the curtains as she and Drew gave them enough material to gossip about for the next ten editions of their papers. The potential headlines in the business pages could be even more provocative.

"I can just see the headline on Gregory Hanks's column," she said, still chuckling. "Merger talks begin between Harrington Industries exec and Landry CEO."

"I like that," Drew agreed. "Care to merge?"

"If you're referring to us, we've already put that possibility on hold. If you're referring to our companies, don't hold your breath."

"It might not be a bad idea, you know," he said thoughtfully, as though the prospect had just occurred to him. "We'd be an unbeatable team."

Tina eyed him warily. Why this sudden talk of a merger? In an instant, Drew had reawakened her earlier doubts about why he had involved himself so deeply in her life.

"I've already got my business lineup in place. I'm not interested in joining a new team," she retorted lightly, determined not to take his idle chitchat seriously right now. Later, she might have to examine Drew's motivations more closely, but for the moment she had to focus all her energies on keeping her household together.

That, of course, was all the more frustrating because the entire situation was out of her hands. She could only sit idly by and wait.

When Mr. Grant and his assistants finally emerged, she tried to read the expressions on their faces, but they were masters of disguise. Looking at them, you'd have thought they'd just dropped in for a pleasant morning of tea and conversation.

"Will you speak to the press before you leave?" she asked. "They've been waiting."

"I'd really rather not," Mr. Grant said nervously. "We're still in the preliminary stages of this."

"Then tell them that. I'm sure they'd rather hear it from you than me."

He finally agreed.

Looking uncomfortable and running a finger around the collar of his shirt as though he were choking, Mr. Grant said tersely, "Mrs. Harrington has been extremely cooperative with this investigation. Our preliminary findings are that there are no violations of state regulations. However, we have not completed our report. We expect it to be available within the next few weeks."

He waved off questions and practically ran to the front door, leaving Tina to field the remainder of the questions. Most of them had to do with how she had met her friends and what their backgrounds were. The society reporters, although clearly somewhat aghast at their lack of social connections, were charmed by Sarah, Juliet and Mr. Kelly. Even Billy managed to delight them with comments that were actually printable.

Just when she thought it was winding up, the business writer requested a last question.

Tina nodded. "Certainly, Mr. Hanks."

He turned to Drew. "Mr. Landry, exactly what is your role in all of this? I understand that you were the one who made the report that brought this situation to the attention of the state."

"That's true. I had received some information which I felt merited further investigation. As some of you may know," he said, glancing at his father, "I have a special interest in the welfare of the elderly. I wanted to assure myself that no one here was being taken advantage of. After meeting Mrs. Harrington and her friends, I am now reassured that I was mistaken and that this is a happy, family-style environment. I regret that I stirred all of this up unnecessarily and brought these people so much pain."

Tina looked from Drew to his father, whose eyes were surprisingly misty, and wondered what Drew had meant about his special interest in the elderly. Now that she did some thinking, he had been hinting from the very beginning, but she'd been too wrapped up in her own concerns to ask the right questions.

Even now, her appreciation and curiosity couldn't dispel the aura of gloom that seemed to weave around her. She still worried about how this could end up and what it might do to the image of Harrington Industries.

Since taking over, she had tried so hard to do the things that she thought would make Gerald proud and, while she knew he would have approved of what she'd done by taking in her friends, she wasn't sure how he would have felt about the implications for his company. Gerald had been an intensely private man who ran his business with quiet diplomacy and behind-the-scenes finesse. It appeared she was about to bring everything into the public eye with a bang.

She was drawn back from her reverie by the tail end of another question from the business writer.

"So you don't see this as increasing the opportunity for you to snap up Harrington Industries?"

Tina's breath caught in her throat as her attention was riveted on Drew, awaiting his response. The question pulled together all of the confusion and doubts that had begun to plague Tina. Drew met her gaze steadily, and his reply was clearly directed more to her than to Gregory Hanks.

"My interest in this situation is strictly personal. It has nothing whatsoever to do with Harrington Industries or Landry Enterprises."

"But you must agree that adverse publicity right now for Mrs. Harrington would make her company a prime target for a takeover attempt."

"As a businessman, I would have to say that your analysis is correct. However, I repeat, I am not interested in acquiring Harrington Industries."

Drew's statement was made with absolute conviction, but Tina couldn't shake the feeling that he was only saying what he knew she wanted to hear. Trust, which had been building slowly, suffered a severe setback.

Chapter Eight

As soon as the last of the reporters had left, Tina sagged against the front door with relief.

What an ordeal!

She wanted nothing more than a day—maybe even a whole month—all to herself to try to sort out everything that had happened, but getting time alone in this house was next to impossible. She would have settled for an hour just to think about Drew's offhand, yet disturbing private allusions to a possible merger, followed only moments later by his public denial that such a prospect had ever occurred to him.

For the last few days she had put aside her doubts about his motives, but his comments this morning had made it impossible for her to go on ignoring her suspicions. With the critical stockholders' meeting coming up soon, she had to find some way to counter all of the adverse publicity. Otherwise, Gregory Hanks's suggestion about some shark—possibly Drew?—sniffing blood was very likely to become a reality.

The one thing she didn't want to face, but knew she had to, was the possibility that Drew had initiated the HRS investigation not for his stated reasons, but because of his own interest in Harrington Industries. Was he actively pursuing her for the same reason? She had to find some way to discover the truth before it was too late.

A thought flashed through her mind. If Drew were making a move on the company, it might be showing up already in the sale of Harrington Industries stock. Checking to make sure that Drew had gone outside with the others, she went to a phone to call her assistant, David Warren, an eager young man who'd proved himself time and again. Not only was he good with the stockholders, but he was efficient, loyal and, above all, discreet. She needed to rely on all of those traits now more than ever.

"Jennifer, get David for me."

"Sure, honey. How did this morning go?"

"Don't ask. I'm sure you'll read all about it in the papers anyway."

"I can hardly wait. I just love starting my day with juicy gossip, especially when I know it's probably not true. Just a second and I'll put David on."

A moment later he picked up. "Hi, Tina. What's up?"

"David, I want you to do some checking for me."

"Sure."

"Do a little nosing around with our brokerage house contacts and see if there's been any unusual movement in our stock."

David's voice dropped to a whisper. "Have you heard something? Is there anything in particular I should be asking about?"

"No. Not yet. I just have a few unsubstantiated suspicions. For now, just check on the movement. Is the volume especially high, any large blocks selling, that sort of thing. Okay?"

"You've got it. Want me to call you back at home or will you be in later?"

"If you discover anything significant call me here. Otherwise we'll talk it over again tomorrow. I want you to stay on top of this for the next few weeks."

"Sure."

"Thanks, David."

When she'd hung up, she sat for a long time, staring pensively out the window, wondering when she had become so distrustful. Would her entire future always be filled with doubts? The possibility depressed her. There couldn't be much joy in success if it robbed her of the ability to trust, to care.

She sighed as she caught a glimpse of a laughing Drew. He, Aunt Juliet and Billy were on the lawn playing croquet. Drew was leaning down to whisper in Aunt Juliet's ear, probably suggesting strategy judging from the scowl Billy was shooting at them.

"Hey, you guys, no fair," Billy finally shouted, his voice drifting into the house on the breeze. Tina grinned at his indignation. Billy did everything with an all-out energy, and his desire to win reminded Tina of herself as a girl.

From a very early age, she'd had ambition and drive. At first it had been evidenced by little more than the typical ten-cent lemonade stand, set up on the front lawn day after day until she'd had enough money for a bright green bicycle she wanted. As she'd grown older, her goal had been refined, her determination solidified: she was going to change her life for the better, to achieve the success that had always eluded her parents.

She realized now it hadn't been so much the money or social status that had motivated her. She'd simply wanted the respect that seemed to go hand in hand with them. In Palm Beach County the separation between rich and poor wasn't a line. It was the whole damn length of the causeway. She'd wanted desperately to cross that bridge, just for the sheer joy of the challenge. Few people made it. She wanted to be one of them.

Billy responded to challenges just as she had. Although life had become easier for him since coming to live with Tina, he hadn't forgotten the past. Last night's tearful conversation had been proof enough of that. Though he had the adolescent's aversion to studying, he had enough street savvy to survive in school and the athletic ability to be a star. Billy would make a name for himself someday. She had no doubts about it.

Tina grinned as Billy moaned loudly when Aunt Juliet, hooting with glee, drove his ball far from the next wicket. Drew threw his arms around Juliet and planted a kiss on her cheek. As far away as she was, Tina could see the older woman blushing with pleasure. When wisps of her hair fell loose from her bun, Aunt Juliet didn't even notice.

"Hey, Billy," Tina called out the window. "Maybe you should stick to baseball."

Billy looked up and gave her a crooked smile. "Why don't you get out here and help? These guys are teaming up against me."

"Hold them off awhile longer. I'll be out as soon as I do something about lunch."

However, when she walked through the swinging door that separated the dining room and kitchen a few minutes later, she found that Grandmother Sarah was already pouring iced tea into a crystal pitcher and arranging sandwiches on a plate. Seth Landry was sitting at the table, his long legs stretched out in front of him, his fingers laced behind his head. As Tina watched, he reached out and snitched a piece of ham that had fallen onto the plate. Sarah smacked his hand. With a sense of amazement and delight, Tina realized that he looked perfectly at home, as though he'd been doing the same thing for years and years. The normally unflappable Sarah was as nervous and fluttery as a teenager.

Tina smiled as she caught the sparks of interest arcing between the two of them. "Need any help?" she asked brightly.

Startled, Sarah practically knocked over the pitcher of tea. She glowered at Tina. "Christina Elizabeth, stop sneaking up on me. You're going to scare me to death one of these days and you'll have that on your conscience forever. I'll probably even come back to haunt you."

Seth's blue eyes sparkled and, Tina noted, he never once turned away from Sarah. The man looked as though he'd been dazzled by a bolt of lightning.

"I only asked if you needed any help," Tina said with exaggerated innocence. She had to try very hard not to wink at Drew's father. "Your mind must have been on other things."

Sarah's scowl deepened. "Just take these things out to the others," she grumbled. "I'll be along with the pie in a minute. It's warming in the oven." Her glance skimmed over Seth, then focused on the oven door as she mumbled, "Maybe you should go on out with Tina."

"Nope," Seth said, settling down more comfortably right where he was. "Think I'll stay right here. Haven't been around a kitchen that smelled this good in a long time."

"Sarah does bake a terrific pie," Tina said agreeably, picking up the overburdened tray of food. "Take your time."

"Perceptive gal," she heard Seth say after she'd left the room.

"I don't know what you mean," Sarah retorted huffily, and Tina rolled her eyes heavenward.

If the last few minutes were any indication, Seth Landry's visit to Florida ought to be very interesting. She wondered if he needed to get back in time for the spring planting or, for that matter, the fall harvest. Sarah was not likely to be won over easily. She had an independent streak that went back more than sixty years and had survived the persuasive tactics of many an amorous suitor. Tina had no idea why she'd never married, but she knew Sarah was too warm and giving not to have had her share of love along the way.

Still grinning at the thought of the fireworks to come, Tina went back through the living room, only to discover that the croquet game had apparently ended and that Drew had come back inside. He was standing at her desk with a puzzled expression on his face, holding a piece of her stationery.

"Who won the game?" she asked neutrally, not sure she was thrilled about being alone with him now that her mind was reeling with confusing thoughts and doubts.

"What?"

"Croquet. Who won?"

"Oh. Juliet did."

"With a little help from you from the looks of it. I suspect Billy's going to be out for blood after lunch."

"Hmm," he muttered distractedly.

"Drew, is something wrong?"

"I wonder..." His mind was still a million miles away.

"Drew!" Tina said in exasperation. "What is going on?"

He looked up finally and caught the stubborn set of her chin. "Sorry. I was just trying to figure something out."

"So I noticed. Care to explain or would you prefer to keep this mystery to yourself?"

"Give me a couple more minutes." He noticed the tray in her hands for the first time. "Take that on out, why don't you, and then come back. I need to ask you something.''

There was an odd edge to his voice, an unfamiliar tone she couldn't quite identify. Puzzled, she watched him for a minute, then shrugged. "Okay. I'll be right back.''

But Drew was already absorbed with the note in his hand.

When she returned a few minutes later, her curiosity fully aroused, he hadn't moved an inch and he was still scanning the same piece of paper. He held it out to her.

"Is this yours?''

She regarded him oddly, still perplexed by the intensity of his tone. "You mean the stationery? Of course. It has my name engraved on it.''

He arched his eyebrow meaningfully. "I was referring to the handwriting.''

Tina looked at it more closely. "No. It's Aunt Juliet's. She was answering some invitations for me. Why?''

Suddenly, Drew's eyes danced with amusement and his lips started twitching. Then they quirked into a full-fledged smile followed by a roar of laughter. "Oh my. This is too much. I should have guessed.''

"Mind letting me in on the joke?''

"We've been had, my dear.''

"What on earth are you talking about?''

"Remember I told you about those anonymous letters, telling me about what was going on here and suggesting that I should check it out personally.''

"The ones that sent you scurrying off to talk to my neighbors and interview every official in town?"

"Yep."

"How could I forget? What about them?"

"We have Aunt Juliet to thank for them."

"What!" Tina's horrified shriek wasn't muffled a bit by the thick velvet drapes. It practically shook the windows.

Drew nodded, wearing one heckuva grin, Tina thought as she tried to focus on the implications of what he was saying.

"I'm no handwriting expert," he told her, "but I'd wager my income for the next few years on it."

"But why?" Tina's amber eyes filled with confusion. "Why on earth would she do something like that? She must have known the trouble it would cause."

"Obviously she didn't." He held out his hand. "Shall we go find out what she was up to?"

The conversation that followed was like something out of a Freudian case study. As soon as everyone had assembled on the terrace, Drew gazed fondly at Juliet and said gently, "Mind if I ask you a question?"

"Of course not, young man. You're practically a part of the family."

"Were you the one who sent me those anonymous letters?" he asked bluntly.

Aunt Juliet immediately turned pale. Behind her glasses, her eyes took on a vague, faraway look, and she twisted her napkin nervously. She did not once meet Tina's incredulous gaze.

"I don't know what you mean," she said in a whispery, frightened voice.

"I think you do. It's okay. I just wanted to know if you were the one who sent them."

Tears welled up in Juliet's brown eyes and she tugged off her glasses and wiped at the dampness futilely. "I didn't mean to cause all this fuss. We only wanted to do something nice for Tina," she said, staring at Drew pleadingly. "I had no idea... Oh, I'm so sorry."

Suddenly she jumped up and ran weeping into the house.

"Now look what you've done. Thought we'd had enough of an inquisition 'round here already today," Mr. Kelly admonished and went after her. Billy glared at Drew, then followed.

"Oh, dear, it's all my fault," Grandmother Sarah wailed, as Seth Landry patted her hand.

"Now, Sarah, calm down," he said gently. "Don't get all worked up over this. I'm sure they'll understand."

"Understand what?" Tina demanded, just as Drew repeated, "Your fault?"

To Tina's astonishment, Sarah blushed furiously and clung tightly to Seth Landry's hand. She must really be in a dither if she was hanging onto a man she hardly knew.

"Well?" Tina urged. "What did you do, Sarah?"

"Leave the woman be," Seth said defensively. "Can't you see you're upsetting her?"

"If she's done something, we might as well get it out in the open," Tina countered. "Keeping things quiet has already caused enough trouble."

"It's okay, Seth," Sarah said with a resigned sigh. "Tina's right. I suppose I might as well admit to everything."

"Sarah!" Tina's patience was reaching the breaking point.

"All right. Just give me a minute to pull my thoughts together."

"Your thoughts have never been scattered for a single minute. Stop fiddling around."

Sarah's eyes twinkled with a devilish glint, then shifted to include Drew. "Okay. The truth of the matter is that I was trying to think of some way to get the two of you together. I'd seen Drew's picture in the paper and you didn't have anyone in your life to speak of."

She stared at Tina, daring her to contradict the statement. Tina simply scowled. "When he moved in next door, I thought it was too good to be true. Juliet and I discussed it, and I guess she decided to take matters into her own hands. You know how she can be when she goes all flighty and romantic. I had no idea things would get this out of hand. I doubt if she ever even thought of the consequences."

"You were trying to do *what*?" Tina still couldn't believe her ears and she didn't dare look at Drew. Of all the hare-brained, idiotic, humiliating schemes.

Drew was suddenly chuckling again. Tina glowered at him. "Are you crazy, too?"

"No crazier than anyone else around here."

"Sarah, how could you?" Tina glared at Seth Landry. "How did you know about this?"

"Sarah just mentioned that she thought something like this might have happened, but she wasn't sure. She's been worried sick about it."

"Why didn't you say something to me?" Tina demanded. "Maybe I could have done something sooner. If I'd gone right over, I could have stopped that report to HRS."

"Like Seth said, I wasn't sure, until now. I didn't want to go pointing the finger at Juliet. Besides, what good would it have done? All the wheels were already in motion. My telling you wouldn't have stopped them."

"Dear God," Tina moaned. "I don't believe this. You two and your matchmaking. I should have known that sooner or later something like this would go on. Couldn't you have tried a little harder to like Martin? Then none of this would have happened."

At the mention of Martin, Drew shot her a startled glance. Sarah lifted her chin defiantly. "You don't have to make such a fuss about it now. It might not have been the ideal solution, but it worked, didn't it?" she sniffed. "You two are together, aren't you? That's all we wanted."

Tina and Drew exchanged glances, hers resigned, his sparkling with devilment. "Not yet, we aren't," she retorted, as he nodded enthusiastically. "Don't you go encouraging her."

"Why not? I think she's got a terrific head on her shoulders."

"You're all impossible. While you're so busy manipulating my love life, the state's going to come in here and cart every one of us off to the funny farm, where," she added pointedly, "I'm not at all sure we don't belong."

She stood and ran around the corner of the house, only to run smack into Martin. The impact rocked her back on her heels. He reached out to steady her, though his gray eyes were filled with disapproval and his mouth was twisted in a way that reminded her of someone forced into doing a distasteful deed. She got the distinct impression he would have preferred to see her fall flat on her rear.

She cursed under her breath. She did not need this. Biting off every word with a minimum of politeness in her tone, she said, "Martin! What are you doing here?"

It was amazing, but until a few minutes ago she hadn't given him a thought. She'd never once considered calling on him for moral support. Now that he was here, she found his presence to be nothing more than another irritant in an already horrendous day.

"I came to see what the devil was going on over here," he replied peevishly. He looked surprisingly rumpled and distraught. Martin never appeared in public unless every hair was in place. He must be upset, she decided, then realized why when he added, "I couldn't even get in a decent game of golf at the country club because everyone kept coming up to ask if you'd gone bonkers or something."

Tina prayed for strength. "Not so far, though I am considering it," she retorted. Martin was staring at her as though he'd never really seen her before.

"I don't understand. How could you allow yourself to become the subject of public ridicule, Christina? It's certainly not good for business and it's an embarrassment to me personally."

If she'd been distracted and upset when she bumped into Martin, his remark got her full attention. "An embarrassment to you? I'm not sure I understand." Her tone would have daunted a more sensitive man. It didn't faze Martin.

"People know that you and I are involved—"

"We are not involved, Martin."

He looked at her peculiarly. "Of course, we are. Everyone expects that we'll get married one day. I'll take over Harrington Industries, if you haven't destroyed it by then..." His voice trailed off significantly.

"I beg your pardon," she said coldly. "You will never take over Harrington Industries, and you and I will never be married. It's not like you to make assumptions, Martin." In fact, it was not like Martin to make a scene, either. Obviously he figured this one was too erratic. He took her hand and patted it. She did not find the gesture comforting. If anything, it was patronizing and infuriated her even more. His words only added to her rapidly growing sense of outrage.

"Now, Christina," he began in an awful, condescending tone. "I realize all of this unpleasant notoriety has been most upsetting to you, but don't talk crazy. People will forget all about this little peccadillo as soon as another scandal comes along.''

"Peccadillo? Scandal?" she said with quiet fury. "You think I'm involved in a scandal? You don't know the meaning of the word. There have been divorces in this town that scattered more dirt than what's happening here."

Martin continued as though she'd never opened her mouth. "You and I will be married as soon as everything settles down again and these people are out of here."

Shock filled Tina's eyes, followed by a sharp twisting in her stomach. "You want my friends to leave?"

Martin apparently missed the ominous edge to her voice because he blundered on. "They certainly can't live with us. I'm sure you can find them a more suitable place, perhaps a nice nursing home for the older ones and a foster home for the boy if you feel you must help them. They don't belong on a Palm Beach estate."

"Why you...you..." Words failed her. "I don't think I ever realized that you are nothing but a high-class snob! How dare you come here and insult my friends. There's not a one of them who needs to be in a damned nursing home. If anyone doesn't belong on this Palm Beach estate, it's you!"

She tried to brush past him, but he caught her arm. "Christina, don't be foolish."

"I'm not being foolish, Martin. I am seeing things very clearly. And, frankly, I don't much like what I see."

She twisted free from his grasp and stalked across the lawn, not stopping until she was off the grounds and across the street.

She'd always believed that the sea, whether smooth as glass or whipped to a white-capped turbulence as it was now, held a sort of magic, that it could bring her serenity. After the HRS inspection, the press conference, her doubts about Drew, then Aunt Juliet's revelation and now Martin, today was going to be a real humdinger test of its powers.

Chapter Nine

Tina had gone to the beach, oblivious to the rolling clouds that were gathering to the west in the late afternoon sky, turning it to an ominous gray. The wild fury of the impending storm matched her mood perfectly. Even when torrents of rain poured down, plastering her auburn hair to her head and soaking her clothes so that they clung revealingly and uncomfortably to her body, she continued to walk, wondering how her life had gotten into such a tangle in so short a time.

As if things hadn't been bad enough, Martin's revealing outburst had shattered her few remaining illusions about his suitability for her. Oddly enough, she felt more relief than dismay. How had she ever deluded herself into thinking that they might someday become seriously involved? Worse, how had she ever thought that he was remotely comparable to Gerald?

Martin had revealed himself as an undeniable snob, one of the idle rich who had nothing to do except make judgments about other people. Talk about people destroying Harrington Industries. Martin could probably do it within a week. That's probably why his father had given him such a large trust fund, to keep him safely away from the family firm.

Tina was rounding a curve of the ocean when she spotted Drew ambling toward her. His hands were jammed into the pockets of faded, cutoff jeans he'd obviously gone home to put on. Those jeans ought to be outlawed in mixed company, Tina decided.

Water ran down his face and cascaded over his bare shoulders. It reminded her of the day she'd caught him coming out of his pool. It seemed no matter how lousy she felt, or what his role had been in creating the events affecting her mood, she was always glad to see him, always instantly aroused by him to an intriguing level of sunlight-bright expectancy.

"Mind some company?" he said as his gaze swept over her with heated intensity, finally coming to rest on her breasts, which were clearly visible through the soaked material of her blouse. Her nipples hardened.

She shrugged, feigning an indifference she most certainly did not feel.

"Want to tell me what got you so upset back there?"

"Before or after Martin?"

Drew stared at her blankly. "Who the devil is this Martin? That's the second time this afternoon his name has come up."

"According to Sarah, he's a wimp. According to him, he's the man I'm supposed to marry."

"And according to you?" he asked with tight-lipped restraint, his eyes darkening to a shade even more dangerous than the sky.

Tina grinned wryly. "I think Sarah has it pegged."

Drew's expression brightened. "That takes care of old Martin, then. What sent you scurrying off in the first place? You don't usually run away from your problems."

"I told you. I'm worried sick about what will happen to those people if the state says they can't stay. All of the meddling by Juliet and Sarah may wind up destroying our lives."

"They love you. It was well-intentioned."

She sighed. "I know that and I'm sorry I snapped at everybody, but, Drew, don't you see? They could be back on the streets or in some dump, and I could lose everything—my friends, my company."

"Your money?"

"I don't care about the money. I never have. What would I spend it on anyway, aside from the upkeep of the house? I don't travel. I don't have expensive taste. The idea of spending hundreds of dollars for a blouse or a pair of shoes appalls me. My one extravagance is..." She snapped her mouth shut and blushed. "Well, never mind what it is."

Drew was immediately intrigued by her reticence. Naturally. "Tina! What exactly do you fritter away your money on?"

"I don't fritter it away," she grumbled, furious at herself for the slip of the tongue.

"Whatever you want to call it then. What do you buy that makes your cheeks turn that attractive shade of pink?"

She heaved a disgusted sigh. She might as well admit it. Drew wasn't likely to give up until he'd wormed it out of her. The man probably would have been much happier in life as a detective.

"Lingerie," she mumbled.

Drew's lips quivered. "That's your vice? Lingerie?"

"Yes, dammit." She scowled at him defiantly.

"You mean that under those demure, businesslike suits of yours you are attired in sexy, lacy little things?" His voice was suddenly tense and he swept his gaze over her as if he were mentally disrobing her again.

Her heart slammed against her ribs. "Drew, couldn't we talk about something else?"

"Actually, I'm beginning to like this topic just fine."

"Drew!"

"Oh, okay," he grumbled. "We'll get back to that later."

"No, we won't." Her gaze locked with his, first in defiance, then in something else entirely. She felt crowded, though they were standing in the middle of a deserted beach. She felt hot, though the rain had cooled the air. But for all of the tension that knotted within her, it was Drew who finally blinked and looked away.

"So," he said, his voice thick and husky, "money doesn't matter to you. It's your grand passion for your husband that makes the thought of losing control of Harrington Industries so terrible."

"Exactly. I married Gerald because I loved him, because he was kind to me, not because of what he could do for me professionally and socially, and certainly not because of his wealth. I was already on my way up at Harrington Industries when Gerald and I met, and he was paying me very well even then. It was enough."

"He did help you along the way, though. He did speed up the process. You have to admit that."

"Of course, but I could do it again if I really had to. I love the challenge of mastering something new anyway. To tell you the truth, I've discovered that living in Palm Beach is not all it's cracked up to be or it wasn't until Sarah and Juliet and Mr. Kelly came along. They're real. Their lives are more than shopping trips to Worth Avenue or luncheon at the country club. Do you know that Sarah and Juliet spend three mornings a week volunteering at a hospital? Even when they didn't have much, they gave what they did have—their time. They know all about loving and sharing and trust. Some of my neighbors love their stockbrokers more than they do their families."

"Are you including me in that group?"

"I'm not sure," she said directly. She saw the hurt that her doubts inflicted, but she had to tell him the truth. "All this talk about mergers and takeovers this afternoon has spooked me. I'm not sure anymore what you want from me."

Drew nodded. "That's fair." He hesitated, and Tina interpreted that tiny pause as time he needed to calculate a response. Shouldn't the truth have come more easily?

"The answer's not so easy," he said at last. "You and I have just met. You've awakened desires in me I've never felt before, desires for a home of my own, a family. I want to protect you and make love to you and show you things you've never seen before.

"I'm not sure how to go about doing all that. You've certainly made it very clear that you don't want to be protected. You don't want to make love. And your experiences are probably as vast as mine. I'm terrified to bring up the subject of marriage. You'd probably scamper off to the Caribbean and hide out until I go back to Cedar Rapids."

Tina heard the raw edge of frustration and sincerity and responded to it. She wanted to believe he was telling the truth, but was it all of the truth or only a convenient portion?

"What about Harrington Industries?"

"That has nothing to do with you and me," he said firmly and without hesitation.

"Does that simply mean you are able to separate your professional and personal life?"

"No. It means precisely what I told Gregory Hanks. My interest in you is personal. My interest in Harrington Industries, except as it affects you, does not exist. I can't say it any more clearly than that."

The cards were all on the table now. She might as well play them out, even if she wasn't sure where the game would lead. "But you said something earlier about merging."

"True." He ran his fingers through his damp, wind-tousled hair. His eyes met hers and pleaded for understanding. "I suppose I was only half joking when I said that. I've already seen how much that company takes out of you, how much it dominates your life. Even now, with all that's on your mind at home, you're as concerned about the impact on Harrington Industries as you are for yourself and your friends. A part of me would like to relieve you of that pressure so that you'll have time for me. For us."

"Someone else may save you the trouble, once the news breaks about my wacky household. My friends and my company may be taken away."

Drew put an arm around her shoulder. Tina found herself feeling grateful for the warmth, responding to the comfort. "Want to hear how I see it?"

"Why not?"

"Despite the chaos that went on in there this morning, the state is not going to do a thing to disrupt your household and even if it did, those people would still be your friends. You wouldn't lose them. You could even find another way to help them, maybe get them an apartment. Mr. Kelly has his own home already. He could go back there."

"And die of loneliness?" she retorted. "I won't allow that. As for the others, they'd never accept charity like that from me. Here they feel they're making a contribution."

"Tina, you could work it out. I know you. You're an ingenious lady."

"And Harrington Industries? I wouldn't care so much for myself, but it's Gerald's company. He spent a lifetime building it into what it is today. Even Martin, who has the business acumen of a sea turtle, pointed out that all of this notoriety is bad for it and for me. I just can't lose control of it. It would mean I'd failed Gerald."

"Don't you see?" he chided. "That's exactly what I've been talking about. Your priorities are all twisted around. You've put business first, albeit in the disguise of some emotional commitment to your late husband."

Tina felt a cold knot forming in her stomach. "You don't expect me to turn my back on my obligations to the company, do you? Would you be happier if I just quit or turned it over to you?"

He apparently heard the frost in her voice and interpreted its cause correctly, because he replied quickly and with satisfying certainty. "No, of course not. Your career is obviously an important part of you, just as Gerald's memory is. I wouldn't want to change that. I just want you to keep it in perspective. Besides, Harrington Industries is not in any real danger."

"How can you be so sure? Do you have a magic wand to make wishes come true?"

"No. You're the one with the magic. I've been watching you in action. You wrapped those media people around your finger this morning. Even Edward Grant was bedazzled by your style and I doubt he's easily charmed."

"Edward Grant was bedazzled because I have more bathrooms than the average hotel."

"Whatever. If I hadn't been sure before, I would be now. I know you can handle anything the board of directors or stockholders throw your way. Trust me. I'm a terrific judge of character."

As her stomach unknotted, she realized with a tremendous sense of relief that she did. Whatever doubts she might have had about Drew's motives had been banished, perhaps only because she needed right now to believe in someone. She wanted desperately—for reasons she didn't dare analyze—to trust Drew Landry. For now if he said everything was going to be okay, then she'd just have to believe him—even if her normally healthy self-confidence seemed to be taking a royal beating.

"Care to come in out of the rain now?" he asked gently, brushing her wet hair off of her face, then cupping her chin between his hands. The touch of his lips against hers was warmer than the sun that had been lost behind the clouds. His gentle touch held a blazing promise and a raw hunger that tempted her beyond all reason. Right or wrong, she wanted all that he offered. She wanted him to banish the cold that had seeped into her bones, into her very soul. She sensed only Drew could fire such an incredible warmth in her that nothing else would matter. Not the past. Not the future.

He led her back along the edge of the water, then turned toward his home, rather than hers. She didn't hesitate. She needed one timeless afternoon with him. Tomorrow and its problems would come soon enough, especially if David found the information she feared he might. Then it would be too late and she would have lost her one chance to discover if the sensations Drew aroused were as unique as she believed them to be. Because of Gerald, she'd learned that life can be cruelly short and that joy was something to be grabbed and savored.

As she went with Drew, never had she felt more reckless, more on edge with anticipation. Never had she simply felt, without reason, without fear.

At the edge of the lawn he paused. "It's up to you," he said. The fingers curled around hers loosened ever so slightly, as though to signal his willingness to release her.

Tina tightened the grip. She could feel the wave of relief that shuddered through him. "I want you, Drew. For today, no matter what, I want you."

"For always," he countered. She put a finger on his lips to silence him. "No, love. No promises. Just today."

His arms went around her then, holding her close, heat spreading from the points of contact until Tina was surprised that in their damp clothes they weren't leaving a trail of steam as they walked through the gate and slowly up the graceful, curving drive.

"Upstairs, love," Drew said, the minute the door of his Spanish-style home closed behind them. They were standing in a large interior courtyard. A fountain bubbled in the middle, and a profusion of purple and pink flowers splashed a riot of hot color against the cool white stucco walls. Tina was charmed. She was also impressed with the amount of work he had done to restore the house which had fallen into disrepair after its previous owner died several years earlier, leaving his affairs in a mess that had taken months to untangle.

She concluded her rapid survey and grinned back at Drew. "You don't waste any time, do you?"

"Are you referring to my invitation upstairs or the work I've done around here?"

"Both."

"The house is coming along," he said with pride.

"As for the other, when the time comes, I guarantee you, I'll use a little more finesse," he promised, his dimple forming as he teased, then vanishing as he turned solemn again. "For now I was thinking perhaps you'd like a nice, hot bath. You're shivering."

"Is that all?" she asked, her mouth turning down in disappointment. He kissed each corner.

"Oh, I think we can work out something else, if you'd like."

She lifted her eyes boldly to meet his as her imagination soared and her pulse raced. "I'd like. But what about your father?"

"I suggested he might want to have dinner at your place."

"I see," she said dryly.

"I doubt it," Drew retorted just as quickly as he drew her along a cool corridor, then up a narrow staircase. She peeked into the rooms they passed, pleased with his choice of cheerful colors and masculine, but not oppressively heavy furniture. In the bedrooms, brightly-striped Mexican blankets lay across the foot of each bed and cool breezes streamed through sheer curtains that billowed sensuously at the windows. He led her at last to a magnificent bathroom with a sunken marble tub, pots of orchids hanging from the ceiling and mirrors everywhere except on the exterior wall, which was open to the western sky with French doors leading to a flower bedecked balcony.

Finally, Drew's remark registered. "Don't doubt it. I saw the way your father's eyes were following Sarah every time she budged an inch and the way he jumped to her defense," she said. "I don't think you could pry him away from her just yet even with the promise of one of those cutthroat poker games you say he loves."

Drew nodded as he turned on the water full force and poured in scented bath crystals. Tina wondered if he planned to join her. The tub was certainly more than big enough for two. The image sent a wave of heat through her that was torrid enough to fog up the mirrors. She tried to concentrate on the conversation and not the sultry, languid setting.

His blue eyes sparkled with amusement when he added innocently, "That's part of it."

"What more could there be?"

He winked and handed her a towel. "He wants grandchildren almost as much as Sarah does," he said casually, then turned and headed out the door and back down the stairs, leaving Tina wide-eyed and choking.

"Drew Landry, I am not going to sleep with you just to give your father and Sarah a baby to spoil rotten," she fumed indignantly and stomped back down the steps after him, dragging the towel along behind her like a child's security blanket. She caught him halfway down and spun him around.

"Not this afternoon, anyway," he said with infuriating calm.

"Not..."

"Ssh," he said, pressing a finger against her lips. "Don't make promises you can't keep."

"Oh, I can keep this one."

He swept her into his arms, and carried her right back up the stairs. "Wanna bet?" he said, as he sat her down in the steaming tub of water.

"Drew," she squealed. "You idiot. I still have my clothes on."

He shrugged. "They were soaked anyway. I'll leave something dry on the bed for you."

He was chuckling as he walked out the door. Tina sent a splash of water in his direction, but it only soaked the towel she was supposed to use to dry herself. The day was not improving by leaps and bounds.

Then she thought about Drew, about the blaze of desire she'd seen in his eyes, the hunger in his kiss, the tenderness of his caresses and the throbbing tension that made her body feel as though springs were coiled inside. She grinned. On the other hand, there was a definite possibility that it could get a whole lot better.

Chapter Ten

Tina soaked in the fragrant water until it turned cool and her knotted muscles were totally relaxed. She stretched languidly, enjoying the luxurious sensation of endless time. It was the first time in ages that she had pampered herself. With all that had been going on at home and at work, she was lucky if she had time for a quick shower before racing out the door. Was it possible that Drew had sensed this need in her when she herself hadn't recognized it?

Stepping out of the tub, she wrapped herself in the warm, oversize towel, then padded across the marble floor of the bathroom to the thick royal-blue carpeting of Drew's bedroom. He had been true to his word. She found a velour robe waiting for her on the king-size bed. She had to roll up the cuffs, and while it was probably a knee-length size on Drew, it fell nearly to midcalf on her.

Standing in front of the mirror, the expression in her amber eyes softened by a lazy sensuality, she rubbed the thick collar across her face. Taking a deep breath, she caught the lingering scent of Drew's distinctive after-shave. The act was thoroughly innocent, yet held such a hint of intimacy that it sent a tingle racing down her spine.

Once she was enfolded in the robe, though, she wasn't quite sure what to do next. Did Drew expect her to come back downstairs? The thought of bumping into stuffy old Geoffrey in the hall and being subjected to one of his haughty, disapproving glares made her decide to wait right here. She walked around the room curiously, wondering what clues it would yield about the man who slept there.

There was a single photograph in an ornate antique silver frame on the dresser. A woman with laughing, adoring eyes and an abundance of thick, dark hair was gazing raptly at a man Tina immediately recognized as a much younger Seth Landry. He looked so much the way Drew did now that it took her breath away. Both men radiated warmth and strength and a certain air of bold self-assurance that bordered on arrogance. Impertinence, evident in the quirk of their lips, was mellowed by a gentleness that was all the more enchanting because it was not expected.

The woman in the photo had to be Drew's mother and, for all the adoration in her eyes, she too appeared strong and filled with an impish humor. It was odd that Drew never talked about her. Had she died?

Were she and his father divorced? Perhaps she had been unable to take the isolation of living on a farm, though Drew had never hinted at that when he'd shared his childhood memories with her.

Tina replaced the photograph and moved on, stopping at the desk Drew had set up to face the window, its top covered with neatly arranged stacks of paper and rolls of blueprints tied into a tidy bundle. Tina grinned. She had known, somehow, that Drew would be organized, that there would be no haphazard clutter, no need for wasted motions. No wonder a man like him had been appalled by the disorganization of her household, the flighty nature of her friends. Left up to him, they'd probably be on a schedule in a week. She shuddered at the prospect. Although she ran her business with a precise attention to detail, she preferred her private life to be easy and relaxed. That's probably why it had been enhanced, rather than disrupted, by her strays.

Tina found a novel Drew had been reading on the nightstand. She curled up in the middle of the huge bed and glanced through it, wondering what kind of book would hold the interest of an intelligent, busy man. In minutes she was caught up in the story, written by a Cuban immigrant, of a man's survival in shark-infested waters after his rickety boat capsized en route to America. It was a lyrical testament to a man's will to live and his desire for freedom. It was yet another confirmation that Drew was filled with intriguing contradictions. She would have expected efficient, informative nonfiction on that nightstand. Instead, she had found the work of a man whose writing was almost poetic.

As she read, her eyes grew heavy. The next thing she knew she was dreaming that she was caught up in the middle of an earthquake. Her world shook violently, buildings crumbled around her and she woke with a sudden start, only to find that the jiggling motion had not been in her imagination. Drew was standing beside the bed, bumping it rhythmically with his knee.

Tina peered up at him balefully. "You need some work on your technique, Landry. That is not a good way to start a seduction."

"I do not seduce sleeping women, even when they are in my bed."

She sat up and tucked her legs under her, her voice sultry. "But you do plan to seduce me, don't you?"

"What if I said no?"

"Then I'd suggest you get that look out of your eyes, blow out these wonderful scented candles you've lit and get my clothes back to me right this minute."

"In that case, I suppose I'll have to seduce you," he said with feigned resignation. "Geoffrey has your clothes. Who knows how long it might be before they're ready." He waved a bucket at her. "I brought champagne just in case."

"French or California?"

"Does it matter?"

"Just checking to see if you're going for taste or snob appeal. I've had my fill of snobs today."

"Then I'm glad I chose the California."

"Are you going to stand there all day or are you going to sit down here and open the bottle?"

"I'm not sure," he said, and Tina detected an odd note of hesitancy in his voice.

"What's the problem?"

He glanced significantly at her legs, which were displayed almost to the point of indecency by a rather provocative gap in the robe. "Unless you do something about that, I'm not sure we'll get to the champagne."

Tina wriggled sensuously.

"Tina!"

"Okay, I'll behave," she said, and tied the robe more securely. She peeked at him through seductively lowered lashes. "For now."

Drew groaned and put the tray he'd been holding on the nightstand. The bottle of champagne nearly toppled over, and the two crystal glasses tilted precariously. Tina reached for them just as Drew sat down. She grabbed him instead.

"Oh," she said softly, as his arms came around her. Her laughter died in her throat, replaced by an exquisite tension as Drew buried his face in her still-damp hair.

"You smell wonderful."

"Are you suggesting I stick to shampoo and forget about fifty-dollar-an-ounce perfume?" she said, struggling to recapture the lightness she was far from feeling. There was an aching tightness in her loins. Her breasts, full and throbbing, were almost painfully sensitive as the rough texture of Drew's robe rubbed across them.

"The scent of your warm skin alone is enough to drive me wild," he confessed, drawing Tina's glance down to the evidence. Tina's eyes met his and she was lost, hardly aware of the instant when he took her hand and placed it where only a moment before she had been looking. A tiny gasp escaped as her fingers encountered denim-encased heat. Drew's eyes closed and he moaned softly. "That feels wonderful! Do you have any idea how much I've wanted to feel your touch just like that?"

His words gave Tina the courage to explore as she'd yearned to do since the moment days ago when he'd climbed out of that pool and stood before her in a proud display of all of his masculine virility. The corded muscles of his thighs were hard, his skin practically hot enough to sear her. A wild sense of abandon seized her as she touched the bare flesh above his waist, then followed the touch with a moist kiss that left the taste of him on her lips and filled her head with the sharp, musky scent of him.

"More?" she asked as a low groan rumbled through him.

"More."

It was just as well he agreed, because she wasn't sure she could have stopped now, even if he'd wanted her to. She needed to know all of him, to drive her senses mad with his essence. Her lips found masculine nipples, buried amidst dark swirls of crisp hair. She teased at them with her tongue, first one, then the other until she could feel the buds turn hard and felt Drew shudder with each new caress. His shoulders, tan and warm, were dusted with an inviting collection of freckles, each one worthy of attention and a mind-drugging kiss.

She touched her lips to the base of his neck, lost in the smooth, pulsing heat she found there. A satisfying tremor ripped through him and then with a suddenness that stunned her, she was on her back, Drew's knee between her parted thighs, his hands braced on either side of her. His eyes, glittering like rare blue topaz, were filled with laughter and a blazing excitement.

"Thought you were going to turn the tables on me, didn't you?" he teased in a husky whisper that rasped along her spine. "I invite you up here for a seduction and you take charge."

Dramatically, she threw a hand to her forehead. "I was carried away. I admit it," she murmured, her voice laced with laughter. "Never again."

"Never?" he questioned, lowering his head toward hers at the same time he began slipping his robe off her shoulders with excruciating slowness.

Laughter died as suddenly as it had begun. "Never," she said, breathless with anticipation. His lips were so close she could feel the whisper of his breath, but still the promised kiss didn't come.

"You're sure?" The question was soft, taunting. Tina moaned, put a hand behind his neck and pulled him down. "To hell with it," she muttered, just before she claimed his mouth.

It was the last conscious decision she made. After that, it was all sensation, drawing her in, tormenting her, lifting her to spectacular heights, then waiting for her to free-fall back to earth before taking her ever higher.

Drew's touch, deft and sure, was pure magic. Perhaps even black magic, it was so devilishly certain, so craftily confident. His eyes revered her, and she thrilled to the look. A hand caressed, and she soared. Hair-roughened skin chafed, and she writhed with unbearable delight. Hot lips plundered, and she burned with a flaming ecstasy. He filled her, and her world trembled and tilted on its axis, never to be quite the same again.

The culmination, so satisfyingly slow in coming, was a wild, demanding thrashing amid passion-dampened sheets. Drew's name exploded from the depths of her soul as wave after never-ending wave of pleasure rocked her.

It was the untamed fury of a storm, just as she'd expected.

It was the magnificence of heaven and the torment of hell and everything in between.

It was, God help her, love.

From the moment that she recognized that, the afternoon was timeless and filled with a joy that was almost frightening in its intensity. Tina had never expected to experience so much feeling, never known her body could respond like a finely tuned instrument, resonant with pleasure.

The afternoon was also filled with lazy talk of inconsequential things, with the discoveries and sharing of new lovers, talk that circumstances seemed to have robbed them of having sooner.

"Drew," Tina murmured sleepily as shadows crept in to magnify the intimacy, their sense of being isolated in their own private world. "What did you mean today when you told the reporters about your interest in the elderly? Did it have something to do with your father? The look you two exchanged was so...I don't know, special. Sad, maybe.''

She could feel his heartbeat still beneath her cheek. When she started to lift her head to study his face, he held her in place and when he spoke at last, his voice seemed faraway and filled with incredible pain.

''It was sad. We were thinking about my mother.''

''Is that why you don't talk about her? You've told me all about the farm and your dad, but you've hardly ever mentioned your mother. I saw the picture. She's very beautiful.''

''Was. She was very beautiful.''

''She's dead? That's why you don't talk about her?''

''I think it's because I can't bear to remember how it was at the end.'' Tina could feel his body tremble and she tightened the arm she had wrapped around his waist.

''Tell me.''

He sighed and closed his eyes. When he opened them again, he stared straight at the ceiling. ''She developed Alzheimer's disease when I was just out of college,'' he began quietly, his voice tense. ''At first, there were just the little signs that something was wrong. She'd forget the car keys or leave her purse someplace in the house and not be able to remember where. I don't think even she realized it was anything significant. In fact, she'd laugh about it.

''One day, though, I came home and found her in the kitchen, crying. She'd been trying all afternoon to remember her brother's name. It just wouldn't come and she had panicked. She had photographs scattered all around, trying to find one with his name on the back. She was almost hysterical.''

"What did you do?"

"Once I'd calmed her down, I wanted to make an appointment with a doctor, but Dad convinced her she was making too much fuss over nothing. He said everybody forgets things. It was nothing to get all worked up about. There hadn't been quite so much attention focused on Alzheimer's back then, so it seemed reasonable. Mother wanted to believe him, so she let herself be convinced. In the end, I did, too."

"But things didn't get better," Tina guessed. Drew sighed and his hand idly stroked her bare back. Even though it was a distracted gesture, Tina was still aroused by it. Her breasts tightened at the memory of where such touches had led only a short time earlier. She pressed a kiss against Drew's chest. "Do you want to tell me the rest?"

"I don't want there to be any secrets between us. Secrets can destroy a relationship."

"That's not exactly an answer. You could tell me later, if it's still too painful."

"It will always be painful," he said and a tear slid down his cheek. Shaken by the sign of vulnerability that he was strong enough not to hide, Tina kissed the tear away. He sighed and met her gaze evenly, his jaw tightening. "I will never forget what happened. I don't want to forget."

"But, Drew..."

"No," he said harshly. "I have to remember so that I'll go on fighting to see that it never happens to anyone else." He gave her a penetrating look. "Maybe you don't want to hear this. It's ugly, and I'm not very proud of the part I played in it."

"Drew, there's nothing you can't tell me as long as you're honest. It's only lies and deception that I can't handle."

"Mother got progressively worse. It was like that case down in Miami a couple of years ago where the devoted husband finally shot his wife after fifty years or something, because he couldn't bear to watch her suffer anymore. Dad was falling apart watching Mother deteriorate slowly, month after month. You can't imagine, seeing him now, what he was like then. He lost weight. He was pale, his eyes always shadowed by anguish."

A flicker of humor flashed in Drew's eyes. "Both of them had always been so filled with life before. It was something so wonderful to see. I had envied them the little secrets they shared, the laughter that filled the house when they thought they were alone."

Then the light was gone, as the memories once more turned sorrowful. "Now, though, Mother couldn't be left alone for a minute. She was dying by inches, and he was dying right along with her. I knew we had to do something, so I finally convinced Dad that we had to put her in a nursing home where she could get the round-the-clock care she needed."

Tina ran her hand along his cheek. "You did what you had to do, love."

"Did we? Or did we take the easy way out? All I know is that the place we chose seemed fine. It was bright and cheerful. There was a garden that was filled with lilacs in the spring and roses in the summer. There were lots of white wicker chairs under the trees. We told ourselves it wasn't all that different from the farm.''

Suddenly Tina realized where the story was headed and it made her heart ache. "It wasn't like that, though, was it?''

He shook his head. "No. It wasn't like that at all. We called almost every day to check on Mother and we always got very specific, professional-sounding reports. We went to see her once a week, on Sunday afternoons. That was the official visiting day. They said it disturbed the routine to have drop-in callers. It seemed to make sense. Mother did seem agitated by our visits, though often she didn't recognize us at all.

"One week I happened to be very close to the home on a Thursday. I decided to stop by anyway. To hell with the rules. It was my mother, after all, and Dad and I were paying the enormous bills.''

A shudder swept through him and he closed his eyes. His voice dropped to a whisper. "My God, you can't even begin to imagine what it was like. I had to wonder if anyone ever cared for those patients except on Sunday. Mother cried when she saw me. I took her out of there that very afternoon and filed a report with state officials. They closed the place down.''

"What happened to your mother then?''

"I took her home, and we hired a private-duty nurse to be with her until she died three months later. Ever since then, I've been working with officials and groups to see that people realize that it takes more than paint and sunshine to make a good nursing home. Dad and I were lucky. We could afford home care. I still shudder to think what happens to those who can't.''

With something akin to horror, Tina said in a hushed voice, ''And you were afraid that's what was happening to Grandmother Sarah, Juliet and Mr. Kelly?''

''All of the anger and pain came flooding back when I got those letters from Juliet. I think if I'd discovered that someone with your resources was truly ripping off innocent old people, I'd have strangled you with my bare hands.''

Tina gave him a faltering smile. ''No wonder you roared into my life like an avenging angel. I'm just glad Grandmother Sarah had that cherry pie ready. It seemed to smooth things over.''

''It was more than the cherry pie, Tina Harrington. There was so much love in that house. I could feel it when I walked through the door, even though you were scowling at me as though some awful creature had invaded your privacy.'' He grinned at her, and the somber mood lifted. ''It was also that sexy little bottom of yours in that sunsuit you wore over to my house and those bare shoulders in your yellow sundress and that stubborn tilt of your chin.''

Her brows knitted, and she said with mock severity, ''Are you sure you went over there to check out the living arrangements?''

''Well, there were a few distractions,'' he admitted, kissing her chin and then her shoulder. He was head-ing lower when she sighed and murmured, "If only this didn't have to end."

"It doesn't. That's what I've been trying to get through that thick little skull of yours. Marry me."

Tina's eyes widened, and she rolled away from him, tugging the sheet around her as she went. She shook her head adamantly. "You don't propose to a woman you've only known for a few days."

"Is that written down in an etiquette book someplace?"

"Knowing Palm Beach, it's probably in the city code."

"I'll check first thing in the morning, but I think you're wrong. I think I can ask and you can answer."

"I did answer."

"You did? I must have missed it. Run it by me again."

"I can't marry you, Drew. Not until things are settled."

"But you will marry me?" he persisted.

Tina grinned. "Maybe. When things are settled. Knowing my life, do you expect to be around long enough to see that happen?"

"If I have to move heaven and earth to see to it that it does."

"That might be easier," she advised.

"Well, while we wait, do you suppose we could find a little time to ourselves?"

"I have an hour between meetings tomorrow."

"Not good enough." A kiss punctuated the remark. It was a very nice kiss. She wanted another one very badly.

"I'm free for lunch on Friday."

"Not nearly good enough." Kisses rained down her shoulder, across her throbbing breasts and onto her stomach. "I need proof that you care more about me than you do about that company."

Tina looked at him oddly, noted that there seemed to be a tightening of his lips despite the teasing tone of his comment. Still, she couldn't resist those kisses. There were several spots that were feeling neglected. "I could stay now," she said breathlessly.

"That's more like it."

"Except your father is on his way up the stairs whistling something that sounds like 'Don't Fence Me In.'"

"Damn."

"Does it help to know that I share your disappointment?"

"Not much," he grumbled. "When you get home would you mind speaking to Sarah about the fine art of keeping my father distracted?"

"If you expect her to do it like this, you'll have to talk to her yourself."

"A game of chess would do."

"Sarah doesn't play chess."

"Wonderful."

"How so?"

"It ought to take Dad days to teach her."

Laughter bubbled up in Tina's throat, then faded. "Oh my gosh."

"What's wrong now?"

"Do you realize I don't have any clothes up here? What will your father think?"

"Unless you go running out into the hallways without them, I doubt he'll think a thing. Now stay still and I'll go get them."

"Drew," Tina called softly as he went out the door.

"What?"

"Try not to get caught with my lingerie in your hands."

"Don't worry about it. Dad knows I don't wear peach-colored underwear trimmed in antique French lace."

"I was worried about my reputation, not yours."

"Oh. By the way, I approve of your vice."

He started away, then he stuck his head back in. "So does Geoffrey."

Tina groaned and buried her face in the covers. She wondered if old Geoffrey had taken a vow of silence. Hopefully, it was part of the butlers' code of ethics. Otherwise, she could very well end up right back in the headlines. Palm Beach society liked nothing better than reading about a steamy romance.

Chapter Eleven

Out mighty late last night, weren't you, missy?" Mr. Kelly said with deliberate coyness at breakfast, his sharp eyes obviously catching the shadows under her eyes. Tina didn't miss the implication of his remark. It brought an immediate stain of pink to her cheeks. She was glad Billy wasn't around to witness this particular conversation. He'd probably start hunting around for a shotgun to go after Drew.

"It wasn't that late," Tina mumbled, quickly stuffing a spoonful of oatmeal into her mouth. Sarah was obviously miffed again this morning. She hadn't even emerged from the kitchen to ask what they wanted. She'd just left a chafing dish of oatmeal, a bowl of sliced bananas and raisins and a pitcher of cream on the serving table.

"You with Drew?"

"Umm-hmm."

"Speak up, missy. Was that a yes?"

Tina glared at him defiantly. "Yes," she repeated loudly.

A sudden glint of amusement sparked to life in Mr. Kelly's eyes. "Guess Juliet and Sarah didn't do so bad by you, after all, did they?"

Tina choked, then laughed in spite of herself. "No. I guess not," she admitted.

"You might want to tell them that. They've been moping around ever since you stormed out of here yesterday."

"All right," she said meekly. "I'll apologize. I was worried and angry, but I shouldn't have taken it out on them." She looked up just in time to see Juliet's nose poking around the door frame. "Aunt Juliet?"

"Yes, dear?" She inched her way cautiously into the room and waited as if poised for flight.

Tina got up and went to her. She put her arm around her and hugged her tightly, her eyes misting as she heard Juliet's sigh of relief. "I'm sorry," she whispered. "I didn't mean to get so upset yesterday."

"It's okay, dear. I was meddling, after all. My late husband used to tell me all the time that nothing good ever comes of that."

"Oh, I wouldn't say that," Mr. Kelly chimed in with a wink at Tina. "Things seem to be working out just the way you and Sarah wanted."

Juliet's nut-brown eyes sparkled with interest. "Really? Oh, Tina, that's wonderful. Have you set a wedding date finally?"

Tina scowled at Mr. Kelly. "See what you've done. You've gotten her hopes up again. Drew and I have no plans to marry."

"No plans to marry?" Mr. Kelly blustered with parental indignation. "What kind of man is he, taking advantage of a lovely gal like you? I just wonder what that father of his would have to say, if he knew?"

"There is nothing for him to know," Tina said firmly, pushing Mr. Kelly right back into the chair he was about to vacate. All she needed was for the two men to start interfering and she and Drew would be standing before a judge with a shotgun aimed at Drew's head. "You stay out of it. I'm a grown woman. I can handle my own social life."

"You're the one who picked Martin," Mr. Kelly sniffed. "I heard what that nasal-sounding, self-indulgent scoundrel said to you yesterday. If you ask me, you ain't got the scenting ability of a bloodhound."

"I didn't ask you. Now let's just drop it. I have to get to work."

"Don't forget to talk to Sarah before you go," Juliet said. She sighed heavily, and there was a hint of censure in her tone. "She's been so upset, dear. I don't think she slept a wink all night for fear she'd driven you straight into Martin's arms."

"You can both stop worrying about that. Martin and I are definitely through. I'll go talk to Sarah right now and tell her that's one thing she doesn't need to fret about," Tina promised.

The apology to Grandmother Sarah was easier by far than she'd expected. As soon as Tina admitted that she'd been with Drew the previous evening, Sarah's eyes lit up with satisfaction.

"You don't have to look so smug," Tina chided.

Sarah paused in her dishwashing and said with feigned ferocity, "You just can't admit it, can you, Christina Elizabeth."

"Admit what?"

"That it doesn't hurt to listen to us old folks once in a while."

"I don't mind listening to you. It's when you take matters into your own hands that I object."

Sarah blushed guiltily and attacked the oatmeal-encrusted pot she'd been scrubbing with renewed purpose. "I'll try to remember that," she mumbled.

"See that you do," Tina said with severity, then grinned and hugged her. "I love you."

"I love you, too, girl. We all do. Now run along to work."

Tina gave her another squeeze, then left for Harrington Industries, dreading what she might find there. As soon as she arrived at the penthouse, she went straight to David's office. As usual, he had arrived ahead of her. Paperwork literally spilled off his cluttered desk. She moved several folders and sank down in a chair across from him, noting again that for a man of twenty-five, who radiated calm professionalism and dressed for the precise image, he was amazingly untidy otherwise.

"So," she said. "What did you find?"

"Nothing."

Her eyes widened in surprise. "Nothing?"

"The price of the Harrington Industries stock is steady. The volume is steady. There hasn't been a single thing out of the ordinary in the last few weeks. I can't figure it out. What made you think something was going on?"

"It was just a funny feeling. I guess my feminine intuition blew it this time," she said as relief flooded through her. It was true, then. Drew wasn't after the company. After their closeness yesterday, the feelings that had flourished, she couldn't believe that he was trying to use her, either. Perhaps it was just as he'd said, and his interest was only in relieving her of pressure. Now that he knew she didn't want that, he would drop all talk of a merger.

"What do you want me to do now, Tina?" David asked.

"Keep an eye on things and let me know if the situation changes. Hopefully I really was all wrong about this."

Once she'd left David's office, she pushed the issue to the back of her mind, knowing that he'd stay on top of it. She spent the morning in meetings with her art department designing the materials needed for the stockholders' meeting. It was after noon when Jennifer came in and stood in front of Tina's desk with her hands behind her back. She was fidgeting nervously. Jennifer never fidgeted unless things were really bad. It made Tina's pulse slow with dread.

"What's up, Jen?"

"Have you seen this?"

"What?"

She handed over the Miami paper. Gregory Hanks's column bore a headline forecasting Dark Days Ahead for Harrington Industries. Tina unconsciously balled her hand into a fist as she scanned the damning article, which detailed her problems with HRS and predicted trouble at the stockholders' meeting as a result.

"We're already getting calls," Jennifer said when Tina had thrown the offending newspaper on her desk. "Mr. Davis was threatening to take over the company himself."

"That might be interesting," Tina said dryly. "Why didn't you interrupt me?"

"David's been handling the calls, except for Mr. Davis's. I had the pleasure of talking to him."

"Get David in here."

He was there within minutes, his expression harried, his tie loosened. Astonishingly, he looked even more frazzled than Jennifer had a few days earlier.

"What are they saying?" she asked bluntly.

"They want to know what you plan to do about the report. They figure it'll be picked up in the *Wall Street Journal* next."

"What can I do about it? The facts are accurate. I can't very well challenge Gregory Hanks on his interpretation of them or on his predictions."

"Damn, Tina. This is going to blow up in our faces. Can't you get rid of those people until after the stockholders' meeting is over?"

Tina glared at him, and David promptly looked guilty.

"Sorry. I just thought it might help."

"It wouldn't. Then somebody would probably write that I'd cast them out into the street. Besides, I have no intention of allowing this to force me into abandoning my friends."

"Well, you'd better do something or you're going to have a mutiny on your hands in New York."

"And here?" she asked perceptively.

David sighed. "No. Not here. Jennifer and I will do the best we can. Just try to think of something, please," he pleaded.

No matter how hard she tried over the next few days, though, Tina couldn't come up with a quick solution that would settle the nerves of the stockholders while allowing her to stand up for her principles. Drew sensed her anxiety and tried to reach her. In fact, he did everything he could think of to distract her, short of kidnapping her.

Each morning she found a fresh rose on her desk. He turned up daily at lunchtime either with a picnic basket filled with Sarah's tempting goodies or gourmet take-out for which he must have bribed the chefs at the best restaurants in town. He was back every day at five-thirty to pick her up. If she wasn't ready to leave, he sat and waited, subtly pressuring her to wrap things up and take some time for herself.

Best of all, he didn't probe. When she walked out of Harrington Industries at night, she dropped the mantle of corporate president and became a woman in love. Not that she and Drew had much time alone to be lovers. It seemed everyone who'd conspired so valiantly to get them together was now just as busily conspiring to keep them apart—or at least out of each other's arms.

Rather than attending a round of parties or going out to fancy restaurants or even hiding away by themselves, they spent their evenings playing cards or singing along to old records under the approving gazes of Seth and Sarah and the others. It had the feel of a slow, old-fashioned courtship, except for those scant occasions when they managed to slip away for hot, stolen kisses in the moonlight. One night they actually outlasted everyone else and played a raucous game of strip poker their eyes constantly darting to the door in fear that Mr. Kelly might take one of his middle-of-the-night strolls and discover them surrounded by cards and discarded clothing.

If it hadn't been for the threat hanging over her head, Tina would have been deliriously happy. Loving Drew was as fulfilling and exciting as she'd imagined. He was tender and supportive, always ready with a pep talk or some crazy gift exactly when she needed cheering up.

Around the house, things were almost perfect. Seth helped Mr. Kelly with the gardening. They both came in to breakfast each morning moaning and holding their backs. Tina had a feeling that there wasn't a thing wrong with their backs that a little sympathy couldn't cure. They both seemed to perk right up the minute Sarah and Juliet hovered over them with hot tea and homemade coffee cake.

Mr. Kelly continued to grumble about Aunt Juliet's petunias, but he planted them just the way she wanted them. Although he blustered and fussed, there was a definite sparkle in his eyes when she threw her arms around him and kissed him on the cheek for doing it. Juliet spent the rest of the day acting thoroughly befuddled.

Whenever she'd let him, Seth tried to win Sarah over. Tina came in one afternoon and caught them dancing, spinning around in a graceful circle to an old Glenn Miller album. She stood in the doorway and watched, clapping enthusiastically when Seth ended the dance with a low dip that had Sarah's head barely two feet from the floor.

"Oh, my, you're making me dizzy," Sarah complained when she was rightside up again, but there was a genuine hint of laughter in her voice. She waved her hankie in front of her flushed face and avoided Tina's amused eyes. "I'm too old for these wild dances, Seth Landry."

"That was a waltz, Sarah, and you're only as old as you feel," he countered in his calm, easy manner.

"I feel ancient."

"You look twenty-two again with your cheeks all rosy."

Sarah scrambled out of Seth's embrace and backed toward the door. "Don't start that nonsense again. I'm sixty-seven and I look it. I spent a lot of years getting these character lines and I'm not going to deny them now. Your flattery won't make a bit of difference."

"I love every one of your character lines. What do you think, Tina?"

"I think I'll stay out of this one."

"Smart girl," Sarah grumbled as she tried to slip away. Seth grabbed her hand and whirled her neatly back into his arms. He planted a kiss soundly on her lips before chuckling and releasing her. "Think I'll go see what that son of mine is up to."

"So, what's the story?" Tina asked when he'd gone. "Are you and Seth getting serious?"

Sarah turned as pink as one of her favorite roses. "Oh, posh-tosh, girl. Don't go talking craziness. That man is never serious for more than a minute at a time."

"You know what I mean."

"Mind your own business."

"The way you did?" Tina retorted leaving a sputtering Sarah behind her as she went in search of Drew. She found him in the yard playing ball with Billy, for whom he was rapidly filling in as a surrogate father. With Drew's assistance and encouragement Billy had even started doing his homework. Miss Maxwell had sent a note home just last week expressing astonishment—and relief, Tina suspected—at the improvement.

Tina watched the two of them together, allowing her imagination to toy with the notion of Drew as a husband and father. The thought held enchanting possibilities. A few minutes later, when Drew slammed a baseball through her kitchen window, she could only shrug. He looked so pleased with himself, she couldn't have ranted and raged even if she'd wanted to. Besides, Sarah came out of the house shouting enough for all of them. She wasn't a bit pleased about having glass all over her counter.

"I'm sorry, Sarah," Drew apologized. Just the same, he couldn't quite wipe the satisfied smirk off his face.

"I should think you would be," Sarah huffed, though Tina thought she detected the beginning of a sparkle in her eyes. "You're old enough to know better. What kind of an example are you setting for Billy?"

"I'll pay for the window," he suggested, and Sarah threw up her hands.

"Of course you will. Now go on back out there and play," she said as if she were talking to a troublesome boy. "Just be more careful."

"Yes, ma'am."

Tina smothered a grin as she sank down on a lounge chair. A few minutes later, Drew came over to join her, nudging her legs aside on the chaise lounge to sit next to her. He was mopping his face and his bare shoulders were slick with perspiration, but Tina draped an arm around his neck just the same. She needed to be close to him, to absorb just a little of his strength.

"Hey, you'll ruin that sexy dress. I'm all sticky," Drew protested.

"I don't care. I need a hug."

He looked at her sharply. "Why's that?"

She sighed. "Where do I begin? For starters David threatened to quit today, and I suspect Jennifer will be right behind him."

"Why would they do that?"

"Ever since those stories hit the papers, the phones have gone crazy. Every stockholder in the country is convinced that I'm about to ruin Harrington Industries. One man even said he'd heard I was turning it over to charity."

Drew kissed her, nibbling lightly on her lower lip. When he did that, she couldn't think, and he knew it. It was very effective as distractions went. Unfortunately, when he stopped, the image of David standing in her office yet again today, pleading with her to do something, came back in a rush.

"David still thinks I'm going to have to throw everyone out of here before things will settle down."

Drew sighed. "He's wrong."

"That's what I told him days ago, but what if he's not?"

"Ah, my love, I sometimes wonder if you wouldn't manufacture something to worry about if things in your life went too smoothly. Your meeting will go beautifully. Take Sarah, Juliet and Mr. Kelly with you if you want to. If they're at the meeting, the stockholders will realize that they're utterly charming and harmless."

Tina's eyes lit up. "What a wonderful idea! Drew, you're a genius. We'll take them to New York with us."

His face clouded over. "I was kidding."

"I'm not. It'll be perfect."

"I was hoping we'd have some time alone up there. Do you realize we haven't had a single minute to ourselves in days?"

"Only too well," she said with heartfelt sincerity. "Don't pout, though. If all goes well, we'll send them back the day after the meeting and we can stay on."

"And do what?"

She gave him a bold wink. "Anything you'd like."

"Promise?"

"Absolutely."

"Then I'll hold you to that."

The day before the meeting all of them except a disgusted Billy, who'd been left with a friend's family, flew to New York in the company jet. Juliet's eyes were wide as saucers when they lifted off.

"Oh, my," she muttered as the ground receded below them. "Are you sure this is safe?"

"Would you like a glass of sherry, Aunt Juliet? It would calm your nerves."

"Why, yes, dear. It is a little early, but I think a glass of sherry would be very nice."

Several glasses later, Aunt Juliet was ever so slightly tipsy and having the time of her life, at least until the pilot came into the back to tell them that they'd be landing soon. Juliet looked from him to the cockpit and back again.

"Who's flying this thing?"

"I am, ma'am."

"I meant now."

"It's on automatic."

Her brow wrinkled in a puzzled frown. "You mean like one of those coffeepots you turn on the night before?"

"Something like that, ma'am."

"Well, I declare. Do you suppose I could come up there and see?"

"I think you'd better stay right here, Juliet," Tina said.

"It would be all right, ma'am," the pilot said. "That is if you don't mind."

Tina shrugged and Drew chuckled. "I think we've made a convert of her," he said.

"Five glasses of sherry would convert a saint to a sinner," Tina replied just as the plane took a sudden dip. "What the hell was that?"

The cockpit door flew open. "Sorry about that," Aunt Juliet called gaily. "I'm still getting my wings."

"Oh my God," Tina muttered.

Drew patted her hand. "See, dear. If anything happens with HRS, Juliet can always try for her pilot's license."

"Very funny."

The plane banked steeply to the left and Sarah got to her feet. "I've had just about enough of this." She marched to the cockpit door. "Juliet, you get back here. Next thing you know my stomach is going to go all queasy and you'll be up half the night with me."

"I'm sorry," Juliet said meekly, but her eyes were twinkling merrily as she came back to the passenger cabin and sat next to Mr. Kelly. "Isn't this just the most wonderful experience?"

"What's that?"

"I said isn't this the most wonderful experience?" she shouted. "Turn your hearing aid back on. You're missing all the fun."

"You call this fun?" Mr. Kelly grumbled. "I'll take my fun on the ground any day. Don't trust these things."

"We'll be on the ground soon," Tina soothed.

"Don't know why we had to come up here in the first place. Nothing in New York but a bunch of thieves."

"Oh, stop your grumbling. We came to help Tina," Sarah said. "After all she's done for us, it's the least we can do."

"Can't see how parading us around like a herd of cattle going to market will help one bit."

"It will," Tina said. "The press has made me out to be some kind of nut for taking you in. That's an insult to me and to you. It implies you're not good enough to live where you do. Do you believe that?"

"Of course not."

"Then it's time people found that out for themselves," Sarah agreed. She glanced pointedly at Juliet. "Just stay away from the sherry until Tina's stockholders get to know us."

"Why, Sarah," Juliet said, a hurt expression in her eyes. "I don't know what you mean."

"She means if you get tipsy like this again, those stockholders will think Tina's operating a retreat for drunks, instead of just a bunch of old fools," Mr. Kelly snapped.

"You are not old fools," Tina said in a horrified whisper.

"Course we're not," Mr. Kelly retorted. "But they don't know that." He shook his head. "Never thought I'd have to go proving myself to a bunch of strangers."

"I'm sorry," Tina said.

"Don't you worry about it, girl," Sarah said, shooting a scowl at Mr. Kelly. "It's not your fault. It's just the way things are. We'll all survive it. Who knows, if *some people* would stop complaining, we might even have a good time."

Tina had made the hotel reservations, asking for rooms on the same floor. She had requested adjoining rooms for her and Drew, rather than the single suite she knew he would have preferred. When he made the discovery at the registration desk, she could tell that he was biting his lip to keep from an explosion that would only add to her worries. She promised herself that once the stockholders' meeting was over, she was going to give Drew the time and attention he deserved.

When they'd finished unpacking, Drew came into her room and put his arms around her from behind. His lips burned against the soft flesh of her neck. "Let's go out on the town."

"I can't. I have too much to do. The meeting's in the morning."

"You're going to do beautifully," he reassured her, turning her around so he could face her. "You've rehearsed your statement so often, I could recite it."

"Would you?" she quipped, suddenly unsure of herself.

"Not on your life. I'm going to be watching you win this one from the sidelines." He kissed her. "And I'm going to be very, very proud. Now let's go out and do something to get your mind off of all this."

"Any ideas?"

He tightened his embrace. Tina's arms slid around his neck as his lips skimmed across her mouth in a tormentingly fleeting touch. "Quite a few," he murmured. "Unfortunately, I doubt that Sarah and the others would approve."

"What do you think they'd like to do?"

"Dad was muttering something about going to Rockefeller Center."

"To see one of the network shows? That's a great idea." She frowned. "I doubt if we can get in this late. There may not even be anything taping."

"I don't think he wants to see a show. I think he wants to go ice-skating."

Tina's face fell. "Ice-skating," she repeated blankly.

"He figures since Sarah's never done it, it would be an experience."

"It would be that," Tina said weakly, then sighed.

"What's wrong?"

"I was just wondering if Medicare covers ice-skating accidents."

"If it doesn't, I'll pay the difference," Drew offered, his eyes twinkling. "It'll be worth it to see them out there." He studied her closely. "What about you? Are you game?"

"Drew, you don't do a lot of ice-skating in Florida," she hedged.

"That raises all sorts of interesting possibilities."

"Do you want to wheel me into that meeting in the morning with my leg in a cast?"

"Nope. But I can hardly wait to get my arms around you on the ice."

"I knew you had to have an ulterior motive. Are you sure you didn't put this idea into your father's head?"

"Would I do that?"

"Darn right you would."

An hour later they were at Rockefeller Center lacing up their rented skates. Sarah was eyeing the ice with a wariness Tina could identify readily.

"I'm not so sure this is such a good idea. That stuff looks mighty hard."

"Stop dillydallying, Sarah. You're going to do just fine," Seth said, pulling her to her feet. She wobbled toward the rink, just as Mr. Kelly held out his hand to Juliet.

"Come on, gal. Let's go show these folks how to do it."

"Why, Mr. Kelly, I had no idea you could skate," Juliet whispered, her cheeks flushed with excitement.

"Oh, in my day, I tried just about everything at least once. That's the only way to weed out the things that aren't any fun. What about you, Juliet?"

A dreamy expression stole over her features. "I haven't been on skates since I was a girl, but I could do a lovely figure eight back then."

"Then let's go to it."

Tina watched the two couples with a sense of astonishment, then looked up at Drew. He was tapping his ice skates impatiently.

"Well?" he said.

"Well what?"

"Are you going to take all night?"

"Drew, I really have very weak ankles. Couldn't we just watch?"

"And hear about it for the rest of our lives? Not a chance."

"Oh, hell," she muttered and got to her feet. Her ankles promptly wobbled like a baby's. She grabbed Drew's arm and hung on.

"One time," she said between clenched teeth. "We will go around this rink one time and then you are taking me into a bar and buying me a drink. A very strong drink. Got that?"

"Anything you want."

Her face brightened. "I want to leave now."

"Except that."

She scowled at him. "Okay. Then let's get moving. If I'm going to break something, I want to get it over with."

With Drew's arm tight around her waist, Tina lost a little of her nervousness. Still, she never took her eyes off the ice, except to gaze longingly every so often toward the gate where she'd be able to leave it. She was concentrating so hard on survival, she didn't notice at first that everyone else had slowed, then come to a halt. When she heard the applause, she blinked and looked around.

In the center of the ice, Juliet and Mr. Kelly, their arms linked, were skating with a slow, easy stride that was surprisingly skilled. Juliet's hair was escaping from her bun and her cheeks were flushed becomingly from the cold air. Mr. Kelly said something to her and she laughed, then twirled around and came back into his arms in an intricate step that drew more applause.

When they stopped, Sarah and Seth skated over to them, and Tina, her fear of the ice forgotten, tugged Drew along as well.

"You two were wonderful," she said, skidding into them and almost knocking them down.

"Whoa, gal," Mr. Kelly said with a low chuckle. "Haven't quite got your skating feet yet, have you?"

"I will never have my skating feet if I have anything to say about it. Where did you learn to do that, though? I'm impressed."

"Oh, there was a time way back, when the missus and me tried just about everything. I'd forgotten how much fun it could be." He gazed down at Juliet fondly. "Thank you for reminding me of those times."

"Thank you," Juliet said, her eyes misty, her lips curved into a gentle smile of remembrance. "It took me back, too."

To Tina's amazement, they didn't sound sad about having the past brought back to them. She gazed up at Drew and wondered if, in years—or even days—to come, the memories they shared would be as happy.

Chapter Twelve

Tina was lying in bed, her head buried under her pillow, when she felt the mattress dip beside her.

"What the hell!" She sat straight up, clutching the sheet to cover herself more effectively than her apricot satin and French lace nightgown did. At the same time she grabbed for an ashtray to use as a weapon. Through bleary eyes, she saw the shape of her attacker. It looked astonishingly familiar.

"Morning, beautiful," Drew murmured and handed her a perfect rose the exact shade of her gown.

"How did you get in here?" she demanded furiously. "You scared me to death."

"You did get adjoining rooms."

"But the door..." Her gaze shot to the door linking the rooms. It was wide open.

"Was unlocked," he finished with an infuriatingly satisfied smile. "Exactly the way I left it when I slipped back into my own room at 2 a.m." He placed the rose on her pillow and tugged at the sheet. It fell away, along with Tina's initial anger.

"If you ask me," Drew murmured huskily, his fingers playing along her bare flesh, "it was a waste of a perfectly good night."

"I couldn't have you sleeping in here with Sarah and Juliet right down the hall. For all their romantic talk, they would have been scandalized."

"And who put them right down the hall?"

"The hotel," she retorted brightly.

"At your request," he reminded her.

"True. I wanted to be able to look out for them."

"A fine job you did of that," he teased. "They were out until four. I heard them come in, giggling and carrying on like a bunch of giddy teenagers."

"Your father was probably responsible for that. I saw him order another round of drinks just as we left the table in the bar downstairs."

"Actually, I don't think they spent all that time drinking. When Dad came in, he was muttering something about having roared through Wall Street like that brokerage house bull."

"Oh dear heaven." Tina put her hands over her eyes and groaned.

"My sentiments exactly," Drew murmured right before his gaze fell to a point considerably below discretion. "Now could we forget about my father, Sarah, etcetera and concentrate on us?"

"What did you have in mind?"

"This."

His fingers trailed along the edge of her night-gown, following the dip that revealed an unladylike amount of creamy cleavage. His touch skimmed over cool flesh, leaving it feverish and sensitive. Her nipples tightened and strained against the silky fabric. When he lowered his head and took the tip into his mouth, a moan shuddered through her. Moist heat and slick friction created a volatile sensation that jolted her heartbeat from early morning laziness into a frantic midnight tempo.

Drew pushed her back until she was reclining against the pillows, open to his marauding hands and the raw hunger of his mouth. She tried to roll away from temptation, telling herself that surely they could wait another twenty-four hours to be together, but when Drew's tongue danced across the flesh of her inner thigh, common sense and good intentions flew out the window. Her gown slid up, followed by the promise of Drew's kisses.

Tina's back arched and the throbbing he'd set off deep inside became a rhythmic demand.

"Damn you, Drew Landry," she murmured, her voice raw-edged with the unexpected passion.

He stilled his tormenting touches, but his fingers remained right where they were. The pulsing heat went on, slowing, fading, but never gone. "Do you want me to stop?" he asked innocently.

Tina groaned and put her hand over his, pressing it more tightly in place. "No." The word came out on a ragged breath and Drew's eyes smoldered in the morning light.

"Then let me take you to the top." Deft fingers probed and sensation coiled deep inside her, an unbearable tension that was destined for a wild explosion.

Determined not to make the trip over the edge alone, Tina fought against losing herself to Drew's will and countered each of his strokes with bolder and bolder caresses of her own. Subconsciously, she knew it was a battle for control and, in the end, she knew she would lose. There was no way she could hold out against Drew's persuasion, no way to keep her body from responding to the need that was building inside her.

"Come to me, Drew," she pleaded. "Now."

"Not yet," he said, leaving one sensitive curve to pay homage to another as the tension coiled more tightly. "Not yet. I want you to let go. Please, darling. For once, just let go."

"Not without you," she said, biting her lips as she struggled beneath him. Then, as her eyes grew wide and startled, her body defied her, spinning away on a raging tide that rose and crashed with astonishing intensity.

She was still coming down from the wild ride, when Drew slowly and gently thrust into her.

"Drew?"

"Now we'll go together," he whispered, his voice husky.

"But I can't."

"You can," he promised and then she was feeling again, feeling the heat, the shock waves as strong as any quake. Her nails dug into Drew's back, her hips

rose in anxious joining and together, slick with perspiration, they responded with a raw, primitive passion that left Tina shaken, exhausted and more in love
than ever.

"That's it," Drew murmured some time later,
propping himself on his elbow and gazing down at her
approvingly.

"That's what?"

"The look I wanted to see on your face before the
meeting. You look tousled and satisfied and very, very
beautiful. You'll knock 'em dead."

"So this was only a sort of beauty consultation,"
she muttered indignantly. She tried to scowl at him,
but her lips kept twitching. "Other people suggest
blusher. Maybe a little eye shadow, but you could be
right. There might be a major market for this sort of
thing. Landry Enterprises ought to consider diversi-
fying, hiring a stable of...what would you call them?"
She lifted a brow. "Studs, perhaps?"

"What a good idea!" Drew said enthusiastically.
"It would revolutionize the cosmetics industry."

She rolled her eyes. "I should have known you'd
like it."

"I like all your ideas."

"Even the one about your getting out of this bed
and letting me get dressed?"

He paused consideringly. "Well, that one could do
with a little work."

"I suspect it's the only sensible idea, I'll have all
day. Once the stockholders get started, I may not be
able to think at all."

He kissed her soundly. "Now there you go again. Am I going to have to start distracting you all over again?"

"I wish," she said wistfully, but she slipped determinedly away from him. "I've got to get downstairs to be sure the luncheon is set up or Kathryn Sawyer will pitch a fit. She seems to think I can't be trusted to put the proper number of forks on the table or something. Will you make sure everyone else is down there by noon? I want them to mingle with the stockholders."

"We'll be there," he promised. "Now stop worrying. Everything is going to be just fine."

Tina went to the closet where her clothes were supposed to be hanging. Puzzled, she shut the door and opened the one next to it. She was not going to panic. There had to be a reasonable explanation for the disappearance of her expensive new suit. Burglary was one possibility, but she wasn't wild about it.

"Drew, my clothes are missing." Her voice was amazingly steady.

"No, they're not."

"Drew, I am standing in front of the closet. The suit I planned to wear today is not here."

"Oh, well, that could be," he said agreeably.

She shot him an accusing glare. "What do you know about this?"

He cleared his throat. "Well..."

"Drew Landry, I have the most important meeting of my life in exactly two hours. I do not have time for one of your games. Where the hell is my suit?"

"I replaced it."

"You did what?" There was an ominous note in her voice.

"I knew you wanted to look just right today, so I got rid of the suit. I mean I didn't really get rid of it. It was probably an expensive suit and I knew you'd be furious if I threw it out, so I just sort of temporarily misplaced it."

"Well, you can just get it right back again."

"Nope," he said, shaking his head adamantly, a pleased gleam in his eyes. "Afraid not. But there is something else in there. You probably didn't see it. The color is just right for you. Emerald green. Remember? You told me how much you like it. I thought it would cheer you up. That dull old suit was depressing. It was exactly the same shade as mud."

"That dull old suit was businesslike. I actually made myself pay nearly three hundred dollars for it."

"Your first instinct was right. That's entirely too much for that suit." He smiled at her beguilingly. "Couldn't you just look at what I bought?"

"Do I have a choice?" she snapped.

She opened the first closet door again with such force that it slammed into the wall. Drew winced, as well he should, she noted with satisfaction. Her hand fell on the emerald-green dress with its tailored lines. The wool was softer than any she'd ever felt before. She pulled the dress out of the closet and regarded it with caution. Actually it was lovely. It was not too daring, as she'd feared after Drew's assessment of the staid nature of her suit. Nor was it overtly feminine in a way that would have offended her desire to appear professional. And, she thought, the color was gorgeous.

"Damn," she muttered.

Drew's eyebrows shot up disbelievingly. "You don't like it?"

"No, I do. Really. It's just that I don't have any accessories for this."

"Yes, you do," Drew said, climbing out of bed and strolling back to his room. He came back and handed her a velvet box, which she barely noticed since her eyes were riveted on his naked body. She finally blinked and looked at the box he'd put in her hands.

"You didn't leave anything to chance, did you? You must really hate that suit."

"I just wanted you to go in there today filled with self-confidence. Now open the box."

Tina flipped open the lid and found an antique gold locket and tiny gold and diamond earrings. They were so incredibly right and beautiful that they brought tears to her eyes.

"The locket was my mother's," Drew said softly. "I thought you might like it."

His words and the sentiment behind them brought a lump to her throat. She put her arms around him and met his gaze. "There's nothing you could have given me that would have meant more," she said sincerely. "I love it and..." She hesitated for just a moment. "And I love you."

Drew's body relaxed in her arms and he pressed her head into his shoulder. "You don't know how much I've wanted to hear you say that."

Tina sighed with pleasure. Suddenly everything felt very, very right. Maybe today was going to turn out to be okay after all.

The cocktail hour and the luncheon actually did go beautifully. The bartender poured the drinks with an unrestrained hand. The chef had created a gourmet meal, followed by a delicate dessert that looked tempting and highly caloric and tasted even better. By coffee everyone seemed mellow. Tina's hopes for the meeting lifted fractionally.

It took only fifteen minutes, though, for her to see how wrong she'd been about the mood of the crowd. It shifted from jovial to antagonistic in less time than it takes an actor to slip into a familiar role. From the instant she turned over the floor to the first speaker, she heard herself maligned over and over again. The speakers' opinions were based solely on irresponsible reports in the media. No one seemed the least bit interested in the facts. Although the disparaging comments about Sarah and the others were subtly phrased, they made Tina increasingly furious.

At last it was her turn. Her knees shaking, she got to her feet and faced a roomful of grim, hostile stares. A quick glance around told her that Mr. Kelly had apparently tuned out the entire unpleasant commotion. He was staring at the modern paintings on the walls with something akin to astonishment written all over his face. Sarah and Juliet appeared shell-shocked, probably more so since only a short time earlier they'd been conversing pleasantly with these same people.

Only Drew's encouraging smile from the back of the room kept Tina from telling the stockholders they could take Harrington Industries and turn it into a playground for business school drop-outs for all she cared. It was not in her to give up without a fight, especially with not only her own, but her friends' dignity at stake.

"If I understand your concerns correctly," she said in a voice so soft those in the rear of the room had to strain to hear it, "most of you feel that my personal life has become a detriment to this company. I'd like to ask you a question now."

Her gaze wandered slowly around the room, allowing the silence to build, pinning her audience in place as they waited in suspense for her question.

"What would you do if your mother or grandmother or an elderly uncle needed help?" she asked at last. "Would you turn them out because an outsider considered them socially beneath you?" Several people squirmed uncomfortably. "That's what you're asking me to do."

Tina stepped out from behind the lectern and walked to the front row. Her eyes met Drew's, drew strength from the support she saw there. She took a deep breath and went on.

"Sarah Morgan, Jacob Kelly and Juliet Burroughs and her nephew Billy are not members of my family, according to the law. I have no family to speak of, not since Gerald died. These people came into my life at a time when I needed love, when I needed more than Harrington Industries to feel complete. They may not have a listing on the society register, but how many of you have that? They are good, honest people, just as you are.''

She glanced back at Drew and Seth and they gave her a thumbs up signal. She gave them a wavering smile, then continued, her voice growing stronger as she recalled the indignation she had felt on Sarah and Juliet and Mr. Kelly's behalf in recent weeks.

''I've read that they're crazy. I've read that they're poor. I've read that I treat them no better than household servants. Doesn't that arouse a specific image in your mind? It does in mine.'' She waited for the image to settle in, then said with mounting indignation, ''Let me tell you something about Sarah, Juliet, Mr. Kelly and Billy, though. They have more dignity and warmth than anyone I've ever met. They're exactly like you and me. In fact, I suspect if you were to look around this room right now, you would not be able to identify them, they fit in so well.''

There was a gasp of surprise as the implications of her words sank in and heads turned this way and that trying to identify the people who'd been made out as both victims and senile old fools in the press. Tina nodded in satisfaction.

''I see that you understand. They are here and you can't pick them out in a crowd. Many of you have chatted with them during lunch and found them to be intelligent, lively and humorous individuals. Would you have made that same judgment about them if you'd realized they were the people I've been accused of harboring for who-knows-what evil ends? I doubt it. It would be too bad, too, because they are people worth knowing,'' she said simply and with heartfelt conviction. She saw the tears shimmering in Juliet's eyes and the crackling, spirited humor in Sarah's. No matter how things turned out, the expression on those faces was all that mattered.

She waited for the murmuring to die down, then said briskly, "Now I'd like to change the subject for a moment and talk about why we're really here today: to discuss Harrington Industries and its progress over the last year."

With complete confidence, she used charts and a multimedia presentation to show the company's growth in size and profits since she'd assumed command. She could hear the rumblings of surprise when she presented the strong bottom-line figures. Only the board members remained stoically silent. They'd known all of this, yet a few of them had tried to capitalize on the negative publicity to try to maneuver her out.

"I know many of you have lost faith in my leadership due to the publicity in recent days, so if my stepping down is what it will take to keep Harrington Industries on track, I'm prepared to do that," Tina said. "This was Gerald's business. He set its management style and its direction more than fifteen years ago, when he opened the first office. I've tried to carry on those traditions as I thought he would want."

She paused and looked out at the crowd, at people who'd once been her supporters and now seemed to be her enemies. She caught an occasional flush of embarrassment. Several people blinked guiltily under her penetrating assessment.

At last, she said quietly, "The floor is now open to any motions you'd care to make."

When Mr. Parsons got to his feet, Tina paled. If he started talking about germicidal warfare, the vote on her ouster would be quicker than an approving vote on a motion for adjournment after a slow-moving ten-hour meeting.

"Mr. Parsons," she acknowledged reluctantly.

"I'd like to move that we give the current chairman—uh, chairperson . . ."

Chuckles greeted his remark.

"I move we give her a unanimous vote of confidence," he concluded as Tina's eyes blinked wide in astonishment. "I admit I'm from the old school, one of those fellas who think women belong in the home so I can't help confessing I'm surprised at the job she's done, but figures don't lie. Those of us on the board have watched her closely and she's done her job and more. In fact, ain't nobody done more for Harrington Industries since Gerald himself headed up the operation and I say he'd be mighty proud of her. We should be, too.

"Before all this nonsense in the press, there wasn't much doubt about her remaining in charge. Ain't no reason to go changing that now," he said and sat down heavily.

"I'd like to second that," Kathryn Sawyer said. "This company has benefited from Mrs. Harrington's fresh ideas, her business acumen and her woman's instincts. All of this other nonsense is immaterial."

Tina might have fainted dead away if she hadn't recalled that Kathryn Sawyer sat on the board of several feminist groups and wasn't likely to turn Harrington Industries over to a man, unless her money was about to go down the tubes, no matter how little she thought the woman knew about setting a proper table. She knew her money was safe.

Mr. Davis promptly asked for a secret ballot.

"What's the matter, you old geezer?" Mr. Parsons demanded. "Afraid to vote your conscience out in public so's we can all see where you stand?"

"A secret ballot's the American way."

Tina stepped in. "Of course, we'll be using a secret ballot. I believe they've been prepared in accordance with the announced election today of our officers and directors. The proxy votes have also been received prior to this meeting."

When the ballots had been distributed, marked and counted, Tina remained as chairman of Harrington Industries and two of the board members who'd been most vocal in the fight against her had been ousted. A feeling of sheer exhilaration flowed through her. She'd done it. She had won them over and she had done it all on her own. It was the vindication she'd needed before she could let her love for Drew flourish the way she'd hoped it would.

That night, Tina, Drew and the others celebrated with champagne and dinner at an elegant restaurant with an appropriately commanding view of New York. Tina actually felt as if the entire world were hers for the taking.

In the morning, she and Drew took Sarah, Juliet, and Seth and Mr. Kelly to the airport and put them on the company plane back to Palm Beach. Before the engines even turned over, Sarah gave the pilot a stern warning to keep Juliet out of the cockpit.

"Sarah Morgan, you're just jealous," Aunt Juliet accused, tugging her seat belt into place around her ample figure. "You should try it. It really is a most exhilarating experience."

"If it's all that wonderful, you can take lessons when you get back home. Just don't expect me to be one of your first passengers," Sarah grumbled.

"When did you turn stodgy?" Tina teased. "I thought Seth had talked you into going ballooning when you got back?"

Juliet's eyes glittered with excitement and she clapped her hands delightedly. "Ballooning? Now that really would be marvelous. Floating around up there with the angels."

"Which is what we might wind up doing if you fly this plane again," Sarah retorted. "As for ballooning, I only said I'd consider it. If it were up to me, we'd stick to croquet."

Seth's blue eyes were sparkling wickedly. "Oh, Sarah, love, we'll have a dandy time whatever we do."

Drew stared at the two of them in astonishment, then turned to Tina helplessly. "What on earth is happening here? You catch them dancing in the parlor. Then it was ice-skating at Rockefeller Center and cavorting down Wall Street in the middle of the night. Now they want to go up in a balloon."

Tina grinned back at him. "Isn't love grand?"

"Love? I think they're both flipping out."

"Now who's sounding stodgy? Come on, old man. Let's get out of here and let them take off. I was thinking of checking out that tattoo parlor we saw yesterday." Her amber eyes flashed at him provocatively. "I thought I might get a tiny little rose put . . ."

"Tina!" Drew's voice was a husky growl.

"I knew you'd like the idea," she said merrily, tugging him off the plane. For the first time in years she felt as though she could afford to be impetuous, to do exactly what she wanted.

As soon as they were on the ground and the plane had taxied down the runway, Drew whirled Tina around and stared directly into her laughing eyes. "No tattoo. I hate the idea," he said emphatically.

"Oh, really? Why is that?"

"I will not have you spoiling that beautiful, silky skin of yours with some weird little pen and ink drawing."

"But a rose is lovely, fragile."

"You're lovely and fragile enough as it is."

"Am I soft as a rose petal, though?"

Drew groaned. "I do not believe we are having this conversation. Exactly where were you planning to put this little beauty mark?"

"Oh, I was thinking about here." She lifted her skirt a discreet, though provocative two inches and touched the back of her leg just above the knee. "Or maybe here." A finger rested just below her breast.

A choked sound emerged from deep in Drew's throat. "Do you honestly want to do this to me?"

"Do what to you?" she asked innocently.

"I'd never be able to see a dozen roses again without getting excited."

Tina chuckled at his nervous expression. Suddenly it gave way to horror. "What's wrong?" she asked, as her own laughter bubbled forth.

"Do you realize that I have a huge rose garden? Imagine what the sight of that would do to me."

She lowered her lashes and looked up at him provocatively. "What?"

He hardened his expression as if he'd decided to do his duty no matter what. "I guess I'd just have to haul you inside and make love to you every single time I ever saw a rose. Pruning would become sheer torture."

"Sounds good to me. This tattoo bit is sounding better and better."

He twirled her into his arms and gave her a hard, bruising kiss. "Get your tattoo, if you like, Tina Harrington, but be warned in advance. I will probably go mad at the sight of any rose." He kissed her again, his tongue teasing at the corners of her mouth. "Any time." Another kiss stole her breath away. "Any place." Yet another left her gasping and clinging to his shoulders.

It was the applause of several mechanics standing outside the commuter plane terminal that broke them apart. Drew looked very pleased with himself. Tina was thoroughly embarrassed. Aroused, but definitely embarrassed.

She coughed and met Drew's eyes. "I see your point."

"No tattoo?"

"I guess not," she said glumly, then her expression brightened. "How would you feel about pink stripes?"

"Pink stripes?" he asked cautiously. "Where?"

"In my hair, silly."

"I think there's probably an ordinance against it in Palm Beach. You'd be banned from the polo matches at the very least. Possibly from the country club and the Breakers as well."

"Spoilsport."

"Couldn't we just do something a little ordinary today?"

"Like what?"

"Oh, I don't know. Maybe take a walk in Central Park. Go to the Museum of Modern Art. Ride the subway."

Tina's brows arched doubtfully.

"Okay, scratch the subway. We could go to the theater. Or find some little Japanese restaurant and eat sushi." He glanced away, then added casually, "Of course, we could also make love."

"Are you saying that making love with me is ordinary?" Tina asked indignantly.

"Never. I just meant that as alternatives go, it was one of ours."

"Not if you're going to lump it in there with sushi and subway rides."

"Wouldn't you agree that our lovemaking has something a little raw and primitive about it?"

Tina scowled at him. "Is this a trick question?"

Drew grinned back at her. "And maybe a little dangerous?"

"Okay. Okay. It's right up there with sushi and the subway. You win."

"I do? What?"

She tucked her arm through his and beamed up at him. "We'll go back to the hotel," she began slowly, running her fingers up his arm. "Get rid of those adjoining rooms." Her fingers trailed along his cheek. "Take the most spectacular suite in the place." Her nail outlined his mouth, eliciting a husky moan.

"And make love, of course," she added as if it were only an afterthought. Drew's eyes seemed a little glazed, but he dragged her back to the limousine so hurriedly, her feet barely touched the ground.

For three fabulous days they did exactly as she'd suggested—making love with a joyous abandon and unbridled passion, interspersed with walks through SoHo to explore the art galleries, dinner in elegant restaurants, drinks in intimate clubs where Drew's fingers were never far from Tina's arm, her leg, her lips. That always led them back to their suite in a rush. Ignoring the complimentary champagne and a basket of fruit that could have supplied the entire produce section of a small market, they feasted on each other.

Tina was so wonderfully sated, so filled with her ability to finally express her love for Drew freely and without complications that she was hardly aware of the series of hushed business calls he always went into the other room of the suite to take.

It was on the third day of the visit that Tina received an early morning call of her own.

"There's something strange going on, Tina," David announced without preamble, obviously unattuned to the sleepily sensual sound of her voice.

Tina tried to bring her drugged senses under control, smacking Drew's playful hands away from their continuing pursuit of all of the spots he'd found that drove her to madness.

"What do you mean?" she said, instantly alert. She gasped suddenly and shot Drew a quelling glance. He stilled his hands, but he didn't withdraw them. Her flesh burned beneath his touch.

"You were right. Somebody seems to be buying up our stock. The price has been shooting up every day since the beginning of last week, and I don't think it has anything to do with the bull market this time."

"Why on earth didn't you tell me before?"

"On Monday I wasn't sure it meant anything. I thought it might be all tied in to the stockholder's meeting. Now I'm sure it's more than that."

Tina sat up in bed, every bit of her attention focused on what David was saying. "A takeover attempt?"

"That's what it's beginning to look like."

"Any idea who's behind it?" She couldn't even look at Drew, she was so afraid of what she'd see in his eyes.

"Not so far," David said cautiously. "Several people seem to be involved, since the volume is high and no one's passed the percentage that would require them to register with the SEC. So far all of them are covering their tracks well. There's no way to tell if there's a link until somebody registers."

"Of course there is," she said. "I want you to make a few discreet calls to our sources around the country. Someone must know something."

When she got off the phone, Drew was staring at the ceiling. She tried to decide if he looked guilty, but finally settled for brooding as a more apt description.

"What was that all about?" he said, his voice casual, his expression so neutral it made her want to shout.

"David seems to think there's a takeover attempt underway." Again, there was no visible reaction.

"I suppose you want to get right back to Florida."

"Actually, no. I think I'd like to make a few stops down on Wall Street."

"I see." Drew's voice was suddenly cool. Tina had already started toward the bathroom to take a shower, but she turned back as his tone registered.

"What's wrong?" She waited for the bomb to drop. It didn't. She supposed that made sense. Why would he reveal himself now, if he were behind the takeover?

She came back and sat on the edge of the bed, her fingers tangling in the dark hairs on his chest. "Drew, I asked you a question."

"There's nothing wrong."

"Don't tell me that, Drew Landry. I can read you like a book."

"I wonder," he said softly.

Tina was inexplicably hurt by the remark. "Drew, are you upset because I want to go check this out?" She hesitated, then said slowly, "Or is it something more?"

His gaze met hers, then wavered. He was staring at the ceiling again when he said, "No. There's nothing more to it. Go. It's what you have to do."

"That's right and it's exactly what you'd be doing if it were Landry Enterprises."

"I suppose."

"You know it is. Drew, I love you, but Harrington Industries matters to me, too. It's a part of who I am. You knew that when you met me. After all I've been through in the last few weeks to stay in control, you can't expect me to turn my back on it now."

"I guess I just thought now that the fight was over what we had here might be more important to you."

"Loving you is important, but so is Gerald's company."

"That's really the point, isn't it?" he said with a bitterness that stunned her. "It's Gerald's company. Gerald will always come first."

"That's absurd. He's dead, Drew," she said bluntly.

"But your love for him isn't. Are you planning to dedicate the rest of your life to his memory?"

Tina felt a slow-burning rage building inside her. How could Drew put her in this position? He was making her choose between him and Harrington Industries. As he saw it, it was a choice between him and her late husband. The whole idea was preposterous. She was in love with Drew, but she owed something to Gerald.

"Please don't make me choose, Drew. I wouldn't do that to you."

"It's not the same."

"Yes," she said softly. "Yes, it is."

She got up and went into the bathroom then. When she'd showered and dressed, she came back into the bedroom. Drew was gone. His suitcase was missing as well. Drew had made the choice for her.

In a way, she'd been prepared for the happiness to die, but now that it had, the hurt was far more devastating than she'd imagined and it only got worse.

In a matter of days Tina was able to exploit her sources and trace the apparent takeover bid to a conglomerate even bigger and more successful than Harrington Industries. It was owned by Drew Landry.

The sense of betrayal Tina felt was more painful than anything she'd ever known before in her life.

Drew, who'd always seemed so supportive.

Drew, who'd professed to love her.

Drew, who was once again trying to turn her whole world upside down.

Tina had never run from a challenge before in her life, and she didn't run from this one. She flew back to Palm Beach and called a meeting of the board, outlining the information she had uncovered.

"We'll fight him," Mr. Parsons blustered. "No question about it. We're not going to let Landry or anyone else manipulate us." He stared hard at Tina. "Thought that man was in love with you."

"I thought so, too," Tina said softly.

To her astonishment there was a look of gentle understanding in Mr. Parsons's eyes. "I'm sorry, young lady."

Tina didn't trust herself to speak. She simply nodded, took a deep breath and asked, "So what do we do?"

"We increase our own shares, pull together the stockholders and block the attempt."

"I'll spend every cent I have, if that's what it takes," Tina said.

Within days, though, the flurry of stock purchases died down. The price stabilized in wait of news about a takeover. To everyone's surprise, no such word came.

"Tina, you're looking downright peaked again," Grandmother Sarah admonished.

"I'm fine," she said, sipping on a glass of fresh lemonade as she sat listlessly on the terrace. It was the first day off she'd had in ages, and all she wanted to do was sit and wallow in her misery. It was time she mourned for Drew and then put the whole ugly experience behind her.

"I don't mean to meddle, girl, but . . ."

"Please, don't."

Sarah's face took on a stubborn demeanor, and Tina knew she was in for a lecture whether she liked it or not. "I'm not going to sit by and watch you be miserable."

"I'm not miserable."

"Could have fooled me," she huffed. "You aren't eating. When you aren't at the office, you're moping around here. You scowl every time you bump into Seth, as though this were his fault."

Tina lifted her eyes at last. "I'm sorry, if I've been rude to Seth," she said sincerely. "I know he's important to you and I know none of this was his doing."

"It's just that he reminds you of his son."

"Something like that."

"Speaking of which, don't you think it's time you talked to Drew? If he trims that hedge back much further hoping to catch a glimpse of you, there won't be a leaf or branch left on it. Mr. Kelly's already having a fit."

"Tell Mr. Kelly to go ahead and replace the hedge."

"That's not the point, Christina Elizabeth, and you know it."

Tina sighed. "No. I don't suppose it is."

"What is the point of all this fussing then? You do love the man, don't you? Any fool can see that."

"Okay, yes. I love him, but *it doesn't matter*."

"Oh, posh-tosh, girl. Of course it matters. It's the only thing that does."

"The man tried to take everything away from me. First all of you and then Harrington Industries. I hate him for that."

"There's a fine line between love and hate, isn't there?" Sarah said sagely. "Talk to Drew. You two had so much together. Don't throw it all away over what might have been just a misunderstanding."

"Thousands of shares of stock registered in his name cannot be misunderstood."

"Maybe. Maybe not. Find out for sure and then make your decision."

"Have you talked to him? What did he tell you?"

"I think he should tell you himself. I'm not going to interfere."

"Oh, really?"

Still, Grandmother Sarah had accomplished her purpose. Tina thought about the older woman's advice all during another long, lonely night through which not even the sea breeze could lull her to sleep. By morning she had made a decision. She had made several phone calls to complete the arrangements and then she ran, seeking a refuge that would allow her to think through how she could have been so wrong about a man she had loved so much. He had overcome her initial distrust, only to prove that he wasn't worthy of her love at all.

Or was it at all possible that Sarah might be right? Could she have misunderstood Drew's actions? It didn't seem likely and yet Sarah had seemed so sure that talking would resolve everything and Sarah knew her pretty well.

She would talk to Drew, she resolved at last, but first she needed time to figure out who she was and what she wanted from life. Could there have been some truth to Drew's accusation that she was clinging to the past, and if she was, why? Was she afraid of the present? Did she fear the powerful emotions that had swept through her from the very first with Drew? Had she instinctively expected, perhaps even hoped, it would end before it developed into something much more, into a commitment, a marriage that would be stormy and exciting, exactly the opposite of her placid life with Gerald?

If there were answers to all of that, she had to find them. It was something she should have done a long time ago.

Chapter Thirteen

Over the next few days Tina worked until she thought her arms would fall off and her back would never straighten out again. She'd run away to Mr. Kelly's house in her old neighborhood. There Tina swept cobwebs, scrubbed and painted walls, stripped and waxed the floors and dusted the furniture.

When she'd finished with the inside and the outside of the house, she went to work on the yard. Mr. Kelly would have been horrified by the state it was in. There were weeds everywhere. Millions of them, if her aching muscles were anything to judge by.

Tina had returned here instinctively, needing the contact with the old Tina and a way of life that might have been less filled with creature comforts, but which, in the end, had been so much simpler. People back then—even those she hadn't much liked—were always exactly what they seemed. There were few choices and they'd always seemed clear-cut, perhaps because she'd never allowed herself to see anything but black or white. She'd never allowed for the varying shades of gray that could complicate life, even as they made it more interesting.

As the week wore on, not only did the physical labor tire her out so that she could sleep at night, but the return to her old neighborhood forced her to think about her life—what it had been and what it had become. At night she sat on Mr. Kelly's porch and looked across the tiny patch of lawn to the house where she'd grown up. Its porch sagged and it was in need of paint, but it was hardly a slum. It was simply the victim of time, old and tired and well-used. It would have tucked neatly into one corner of her Palm Beach estate and yet, she was just now realizing, it had held just as much love. She was only beginning to understand that nothing else really mattered.

As a child, she had wanted so much more. She used to sit in this same rocking chair next to Mr. Kelly and tell him about her dream of being somebody someday. People were going to seek her out because she was so smart. They wouldn't be able to ignore her as they did the scrawny little kid who wore secondhand clothes from the church rummage sale and talked with a halting shyness.

She'd wanted success and recognition not just for herself, she'd always thought, but for her parents. They'd worked so hard and deserved better than what they'd been given. Now she had to face the possibility that perhaps she'd been thoroughly selfish after all, driven to distance herself from roots of which she was ashamed.

She dug her hands into the dirt to get at the roots of the weeds and wondered if she could get to the source of her problems as easily. Had it been the money—the so-called root of all evil—after all? Had the money itself, rather than the challenge of getting it, tantalized her in ways she'd never realized? That was certainly what Drew thought.

"Damn," she muttered, yanking up a clump of weeds and tossing them over her shoulder. What did it matter to her what Drew Landry thought? He'd only been using her. The pain she thought she'd seen in his eyes when he was convinced she'd chosen Harrington Industries over him must have been another lie. If her priorities were out of kilter, his were worse. He'd betrayed her love to get what he wanted. Disillusionment had sunk in and become her constant, discomforting companion.

"I will not think about that man for another single minute," she swore valiantly, but his image didn't vanish as she might have liked. It lingered on to tease and torment her like a sun-kissed spring breeze that only hinted of warmer weather. She remembered the pain, but she also remembered the moments of incredible tenderness, of loving protectiveness and of blinding passion.

When she'd first returned to the neighborhood after Mr. Kelly had agreed to let her fix the place up so he could sell it, she'd been so sure she would feel desperately alone, even more so than she had after Gerald's death. It was a sensation she craved. She had to discover if she could learn to live quietly, with only her own thoughts for company as she'd been unable to do three years earlier.

In the beginning, it had been difficult. She'd missed the commotion of home—Sarah's wise counsel, Juliet's sweetly innocent humor, Mr. Kelly's grumpiness, their quiet evenings of Scrabble and gin rummy. Most of all, she'd missed having Billy tagging around after her, plaguing her with questions about life and a world that always seemed just beyond his reach.

After a few days, though, she'd grown comfortable with her own company and that of a straggly marmalade cat. She'd piteously meowed her way into Tina's heart and slurped up an entire quart of milk before sprawling contentedly on the sunny front porch.

With only Samantha Junior, as she called the cat, for companionship, Tina tried to analyze her relationship with Drew and with Gerald before him. Both were men of power and single-minded purpose. Both had a vitality that attracted her, but now she wondered why she had been drawn to such strength when she'd only come to resent it when it was used to protect her.

Both men were similar in other respects as well. Both had offered her their faith in her abilities—or so she had thought. Both had given her freely of their love, but again had it only seemed so? She had never had any cause to doubt Gerald's feelings for her, but she now had every reason to question Drew's, despite Sarah's seeming faith in him.

"Mind some company?" Drew's voice startled her just as she pulled another handful of weeds out of the dry soil and tossed them haphazardly over her shoulder. She looked up in time to see the messy clump land squarely in the middle of the pale blue polo shirt that hugged his broad chest.

"Is that your answer?" he teased lightly, though his blue eyes were very solemn. He looked vulnerable, something she'd never have expected from the confident Drew Landry she'd grown to love over the last few weeks. She was astonished to find that the familiar surge of desire roared through her at the sight of him. Her eyes drank in the expression in his eyes, the tilt of his lips, and worry tugged at her heart when she saw how haggard and drawn he looked.

So, she thought, she loved him still, after all, no matter what he had done. She was determined, though, not to let him see her response. At least not until she had some answers and maybe not even then. She started with the easiest question.

"How did you find me?" Her voice was cool, detached, though her insides were churning with misery at the knowledge that she still cared when she felt so strongly that she shouldn't.

"Dad wormed it out of Sarah."

"I didn't tell Sarah."

"Who'd gotten it out of Juliet."

Tina's eyes were twinkling now, despite herself, as she concluded for him, "Who'd gotten it straight from Mr. Kelly."

"Maybe he talks in his sleep as well as taking midnight strolls," Drew suggested with a shrug. "Now that I'm here, do you want to talk about what happened?"

Tina shook her head. "I'm still not convinced we have anything to talk about. It all seems pretty clear."

"Assumptions are a lousy way to communicate, Tina. Tell me what you think you see."

"For some reason, you chose to go behind my back to try to take Harrington Industries away from me. Sarah seems to think you had your reasons and they were valid."

"And you? Don't you want to know what those reasons were?"

"I know what they were. You're a smart businessman. It was a good deal, an ideal opportunity for you to expand your own company's holdings. We're ahead of the industry in the development of the laser chip. In your position, I might have done the same thing knowing all that you did about Harrington Industries and its growth potential."

She stared at him bitterly. "Things I'd confided to you like an innocent little lamb. You must have been laughing hysterically all the way to your broker's."

Drew couldn't have looked any more shocked if she'd slapped him. "If you believe that, then you did a lousy investigation," he snapped impatiently, then clamped his mouth shut. When he was in control again, he said softly, "You also don't have very much faith in my love."

"My investigation was very thorough, but you're right about one thing. I don't have much faith in us anymore. Can you blame me?" she inquired.

"No. I don't suppose so, since you don't have all the facts." His voice was heavy with censure. "But I thought you might at least listen to the truth. Sarah seemed to think you were ready."

Tina sighed. "Okay. Talk. But it won't change anything."

"Perhaps not, but at least you'll know exactly what happened, instead of cutting me out of your life for all the wrong reasons."

"You were the one who walked out on me in New York," she reminded him.

Drew met her gaze evenly. "That was foolish. No matter how upset I was about the choice you made that morning. I should have stayed and talked it out. I'm sure leaving only made me look more guilty in your eyes."

"It certainly didn't help your case."

"Your running away hasn't helped either."

"It's helped me find some answers about myself."

"For example?"

"Maybe I have let my love for Gerald come between us. I didn't mean for that to happen, but a part of me was afraid of the depth of my feelings for you. I was scared by the intensity, by the power you had over me. You're so strong, so self-confident and protective. I thought I might get lost, let you simply take over."

"Did you really believe that could happen? You're the most independent woman I've ever known. No one will ever rob you of that. Not even me." He touched a finger to her cheek and a throbbing heat warmed her blood. "It's a funny thing about needing someone. I'd never realized until that morning in New York how badly I wanted you to need me. I'd always equated that with love.''

Tina shot him a puzzled glance. ''But I'd told you that I loved you.''

''Yes, but when you were in trouble, when David called about the takeover attempt, you didn't turn to me. You hopped out of that bed, where we'd just spent the night making love, and set off alone to do whatever needed to be done. Not once did you ask me to come with you, to help you. You didn't want or need my advice.''

''That's true,'' Tina said slowly. ''I never really thought about it. For so many years now I've been on my own. I've had to do things for myself. My parents weren't able to help me with school. I did it myself, working nights and weekends at two jobs. When I got out of college, I didn't have terrific connections like many of my classmates. I had to be better than the rest of them just to get a chance. For just a little while with Gerald I let down my guard. I relied on someone else.''

Her eyes met Drew's and they were filled with pain. ''And then he died. I don't think I realized until just now that I must have subconsciously decided never again to count on anyone. I set myself up to be the strong one in any relationship.''

''Could it be that's why you also felt so helpless in this crisis with HRS, because for once you weren't in charge?''

''I'm sure that had a lot to do with it. I wanted to fix it, to make it right and I couldn't. I felt powerless, just the way I did when I was a kid. I remember once trying to tell someone I'd seen an accident, but they kept brushing me off. When the police started questioning people, I tried to tell them, but it was like I didn't exist or couldn't be trusted."

"Did it occur to you that it was because you were a child, not because of who you were?"

"I realize that now, but then I just remember feeling this terrible anger and frustration. I felt the same way when Edward Grant wouldn't listen to me."

"But you wouldn't let yourself ask for help? Not even from me?"

"Especially not from you. My feelings for you were already more than I could deal with. I was terrified of reaching out to you and finding that you'd gone."

"I'm not going anywhere, Tina."

"You can't guarantee that, Drew. Things happen. Feelings change."

"And strong people cope."

Tina sighed. "I'm not sure I could cope again."

"You could if you had to."

"But could you deal with the fact that I won't ever rely on you for everything?"

"As long as you needed my love, I think I could handle it. I had a lot of time to think during the last few weeks. I've realized that need and love aren't the same after all. I just want a chance to show you that, to prove to you that I can love you without smothering you."

Tina shook her head. "I don't know, Drew. There are so many things we haven't resolved. This stock business, for example. I can't just forget about that."

"I wouldn't even want you to. I'm ready to tell you everything, if you're willing to listen."

"I told you I would."

Drew nodded and sat down on a porch step, his elbows propped on his knees, his chin resting in his hands. He watched her, his eyes boldly lingering, until Tina felt as though she'd left her clothes inside. It was a penetrating gaze, as if he might be measuring just how much she'd be willing to believe.

"I was not behind the takeover attempt," he said at last.

Anger ripped through her at the blatant lie. Even now, he was just giving her more lies.

"Oh, please." Her voice was thick with disgust and fury.

"Wait," he said, holding up a hand to wave off her expression of outraged disbelief. "I wasn't. Not at first. When I heard about it, right before the stockholders' meeting, I started using some of my resources to buy up stock on your behalf. If you'll check, you'll see that all of the shares have been transferred into your name."

"Sure. Now they are. You did that after you knew I was on to you."

"If you're talking about the date on them, yes. If you think that's the reason, you're wrong. They were always meant for you."

"Why should I believe that?"

"If I were only interested in Harrington Industries, as you seem to think, why would I give it up now?" he asked reasonably. "I have the stock, but there was no move toward a takeover. You know that."

He had a point, Tina had to admit. If he'd wanted her company and didn't give a damn about her, why would he have transferred the stock to her, rather than forcing the takeover? Was he trying to throw her off guard so he could regain her trust and take complete control in a less public way? That explanation was so convoluted even she could see it was laughable. Was it possible that he really had done it all for her?

She sighed and jabbed the trowel she was holding into the ground with such force that Drew winced. Oh, Lord, why did things have to be so confusing? She wanted so badly to believe in him, but the last few weeks had taken their toll. Trust, slow to build in the first place, had died.

"Sorry," she said finally. "I don't buy it."

"It's the truth. Put your best people on it, if you like. You'll find that a Texas billionaire with a flair for hit-and-run moves started buying your stock three days before your stockholders' meeting. When your stock started moving, my broker mentioned it to me. He thought I might want to get in on the action."

"Which you couldn't wait to do."

"You're right. David *had* been checking the stock movement, but when I realized that both you and he were so preoccupied with the stockholders' meeting and that you weren't alert to what was happening on the market, I took action," he said, then paused to add emphasis. *"But only to protect your interests."*

"Why the hell didn't you just tell me what was going on, instead of jumping into the fray yourself? I could have dealt with it, if I'd known the truth."

His lips quirked in a rueful smile. "That's the tough one. I suppose I was being selfish and protective and a whole bunch of chauvinistic things. I thought maybe for once I could do something for you. And once that stockholders' meeting was over, I wanted your mind on me while we were in New York, not on Harrington Industries. I'm not as strong or as self-confident as you think. I'm only human, and in some twisted way that company always made me feel as though I were competing with the ghost of Gerald Harrington."

Tina searched his eyes and found them filled with vulnerability. His jealousy of Gerald was something he'd hinted at before, but only now was she realizing how deep his fear of losing her or sharing her had run.

She put a hand on his arm and felt the muscles quiver and knot. "I told you this in New York, Drew. Gerald is dead. I'm not the type to live forever in the past."

"I didn't say my reaction was rational. I said it was human." He gazed into her eyes. "Before I go, I just want you to remember one thing: what I did was out of love. It might have been wrong and it might not seem that way, but I swear to you it was out of love."

He turned to leave. He was all the way at the end of the walk, his shoulders slumped in dejection, when Tina called out to him.

"Drew."

He turned, and hope flickered in his eyes. "Yes?"

"Stay."

"Why?"

"I want to try."

He didn't move an inch, but hope and desire burned more brightly in his eyes. "Try?" he repeated softly.

She nodded. "I must be crazy, but I haven't been able to think of anything else in days. As much as I didn't want to, I still love you. I want us to get back what we had before, if we can."

"And then?"

"No promises, Drew. I can't make them."

"Will you come back home?"

"Not yet. I think we need some time alone."

"Here?"

"This place may not be the answer either. I think I've made my peace with my childhood. Now I need to make my peace with you."

"Then let's go to my farm in Ocala. There won't be any distractions, and we can start over again. We can get all our problems out in the open and work on them one by one."

Tina grinned. "I knew your obsession with organization wouldn't lie idle for long."

"Do you object?"

"Not strenuously. Just put it to work on something useful."

"Such as?"

"Making the arrangements for the trip."

They flew to Orlando the next morning and were picked up by Drew's farm manager. By afternoon, Tina was riding a gentle filly around the farm.

"Drew, I am not wild about this," she said from the unsteady perch on the horse's back. Her rear end already felt as if she'd been paddled.

"Don't be silly. She's not going to hurt you."

"She may not bite me, but she's in a terrific position to dump me on my already painful derriere. Don't you care about that?"

"I thought you wanted me to stop being overly protective."

"You picked a fine time to go along with me on that," she grumbled as she bounced along the lane that wound through Drew's small orange grove.

Tina forgot all about the aches and pains a few hours later when Drew ran another steamy bath for her, then joined her in it. The man seemed to have a penchant for enormous tubs that accommodated two, even when their interest strayed from the simple act of bathing, which it did often and with astonishingly sensual results.

Late one night at the end of the week, when Tina was curled sleepily against Drew's side, her head resting on his shoulder, the phone rang.

"Ignore it," she suggested.

"You know I can't do that." He picked up the receiver, spoke briefly to the caller, then handed over the phone. "It's Sarah."

Tina sat up in bed. "Hi, Sarah. What's up?" Her face promptly clouded over.

"What's wrong?" Drew demanded.

"It's Billy."

"Is he sick? In trouble? What?"

"Hush a minute and I'll find out," she told him. "Go on, Sarah."

Tina listened, then began chuckling. "Okay. We'll be watching for him. I'll call you when he gets here."

"Billy's coming here?"

"Yes, and I'd suggest you prepare yourself."

"For what?"

"It seems he has a few questions about your intentions. Sarah tried to stop him, but he went sneaking off to the bus station tonight. He should be here in a few hours."

"Terrific."

Tina laughed at the expression of frustration on Drew's face. "Oh, don't be such a sourpuss. Maybe this is just what we need."

"I don't know about you, but I do not need a thirteen-year-old trying to manage my life."

"Not even if he's going to force us to face our situation and make some decisions?"

Drew's eyes widened appreciably at that. "Is that what he's going to do?"

"I'd say so, and unless you want him to make the decisions for us, we'd better start talking."

"Okay. I need to ask you something."

"I thought you might," she said, beginning an utterly fascinating exploration of Drew's right arm. She'd begun at the strong curve of his shoulder, worked her way along his muscled biceps, traced the blue pattern of blood vessels that ran along the soft skin of his inner arm, rubbed the dark hairs that shadowed his forearm and sucked delicately—and she'd thought provocatively—at each fingertip. She must be doing something wrong, since he seemed intent on going ahead with the conversation, rather than using the little time they had for more pleasurable pursuits.

"Have you checked on the stock transfer?"

Startled, she dropped his hand and shook her head. "Why not?"

She sighed, reluctantly conceding that her amorous intentions had been waylaid. "It doesn't seem important anymore. I've proved I can run Harrington Industries, that Gerald's judgment in me was not misplaced. I finally realize that I don't need to prove anything anymore. If Harrington Industries and Landry Enterprises were to merge, it wouldn't be the end of the world. In fact, it might be very smart."

"As a matter of fact, it would be. My computer division's research would blend in beautifully with what you've already done. We'd become a major force to reckon with in that market." At the flash of distrust in her eyes, he grinned. His hands cupped her face, and blue eyes gazed earnestly into amber. "But for the moment, I'm not the least bit interested in Harrington Industries. That's your decision. I'm more concerned with a merger of another sort."

"What's that?"

"Are you ready to talk about marriage? Like you said, we'd better do it before Billy arrives on our doorstep."

"In the general sense or the specific? Generally, I think it's a positive move, if made by two people who truly love each other and know the risks and are willing to work at the commitment."

"What about specifically? Will you marry me? The time we were separated was the worst time in my life. I don't ever want to be without you again. I can't swear to you that I won't try to fight your battles for you on occasion, but I'll respect your right to tell me to butt out.''

"That seems like a reasonable compromise," she conceded with an impish grin. "The only issue remaining is whether you'll actually butt out.''

He hesitated. "Well..."

"Drew," she said ominously, her eyes clouding.

"If it's in your best interests."

"Not good enough. I'm entitled to make my own mistakes."

"Okay. Fine," he growled. "Make all the mistakes you want. I won't say a word."

"Of course you will," she said confidently. "You're bound to say I told you so. You won't be able to resist."

"Can you live with that?"

She sighed. "I love you. I suppose I'll have to. See how good I am about compromising."

"I think I must have missed that part. Exactly how do you plan to compromise?"

Tina pondered the question for a moment, then brightened. "I know. I'll give that suit you hate to Goodwill."

"What a girl," he said, rolling his eyes as he enfolded her in his embrace.

"But I'm yours," she reminded him.

"Yes," he said, his lips hot and urgent against hers. "Yes, you definitely are."

Before they could get too engrossed in each other, the doorbell rang. Drew moaned. "We're going to have to work on that kid's timing."

They wrapped themselves in robes and went to the door together. Billy's eyes widened when he took in their rumpled appearance, and his hands balled into fists.

"I knew it," he growled, glaring at Drew. "You lied to me."

"I never lied to you."

"All that talk about commitment and stuff, it was a bunch of bull."

"Watch your language," Drew said sternly.

"Says who?"

"Says my fiancé," Tina inserted before the two could square off into a boxing stance and start throwing punches.

A glimmer of light sparked in Billy's eyes. "You're going to get married?"

"As soon as possible," Drew confirmed.

"That means you'll be my dad?"

"More or less."

"Oh, wow, that's terrific!"

"I'm glad you approve," Tina said dryly. "Now there's a little matter of your running away from home to discuss."

"I didn't exactly run away. I told Grandmother Sarah and Aunt Juliet I was coming."

"And they told you not to."

Billy shuffled his feet uneasily. "Well . . ."

"Exactly."

"What would be a suitable punishment?" Drew asked.

Billy's expression brightened. "You mean I get to choose?"

Tina shot a disbelieving look at Drew. "That's a rather unusual form of justice."

"These are unusual circumstances. The boy was looking out for your honor, after all."

"That's true," she conceded with a sudden grin. "So, Billy, what's it to be?"

"How about me being the best man at the wedding?"

"That's a punishment?" Drew and Tina said in unison.

"Sure. I'll have to wear a dumb tuxedo."

"Sounds to me like the punishment fits the crime," Drew agreed. He regarded Tina hopefully. "Unless we elope and get married by a justice of the peace."

"Not a chance."

Drew and Billy exchanged put-upon glances. "Women!"

Tina put her hands on her hips and stared Drew down. "Take it or leave it."

"I'll take it."

"I thought you might." She grinned at Drew. "Why don't you find Billy a place to sleep, while I call Sarah and let her know he's okay?"

"I could probably find my own room," Billy offered, suddenly staring at the floor. "I mean if you all have stuff you want to do or something."

"That's okay," Drew said. "We have a whole lifetime ahead of us to do stuff."

He stopped at the doorway and gazed back at Tina, a long, slow look that ended in a provocative wink. Her heart slammed against her ribs.

A whole lifetime. It might not be nearly long enough.

Epilogue

The announcement of an early-spring wedding between industry tycoon Drew Landry and his new business partner, Christina Elizabeth Harrington, set Palm Beach society on its collective ear.

Columnists in the society newspaper speculated about exactly how the eccentric widow with the quirky sense of humor had captured the heart of the community's most eligible bachelor after they'd gotten off to such a rocky, controversial start.

Women who hadn't said a word to Tina since Gerald's death suddenly called with invitations to have the mouth-watering *Aubergines Farcie au chevre* at Café L'Europe or the raw bar delicacies at Charley's Crab by the ocean. What they wanted in return was titillating information. Tina declined on all counts.

Even though the event was to take place after the official winter season ended, invitations were in more demand than those to the annual height-of-the-season Red Cross fundraiser, probably due to an expectation that the ceremony would be something out of the ordinary. Tina suspected that half the town was hoping she'd have the cats trailing down the aisle as bridesmaids.

Partly because she delighted in the idea of keeping gossips guessing, but mostly because she wanted to keep it simple and intimate, Tina restricted the ceremony to family and special friends only.

The wedding was held on the Harrington estate under a cloudless blue sky on the first Saturday in April. Sarah cried, dabbing at her eyes with one of her lilac-scented hankies, as she served a breakfast of waffles and bacon to the excited members of the household. Juliet forgot all about being in mourning and came down for breakfast that day in a lovely dusty-blue dress. Mr. Kelly had turned the lawn into a carpet of lush green velvet and the gardens were filled with bright, fragrant blossoms. In deference to Drew's allergies, the cats had been locked inside. The bride wore an apricot silk dress beaded with pearls and carried a bouquet of apricot roses and baby's breath. The solemnly spoken wedding vows were lifted on the wind and carried away to mingle with the ocean's timeless roar.

The destination of the honeymoon was practically a state secret, at least until Seth told Sarah, who told Juliet and on and on until half the town knew that Tina and Drew were spending their days on a beach in

Monte Carlo, their evenings in a glamorous casino and their nights in a romantic villa on a cliff overlooking the sea.

On the last day of the honeymoon, Tina called home to check on things and found Sarah bubbling with exciting news.

"Mr. Grant was here yesterday. The HRS report is finished and everything's just fine. We can stay."

"Oh, Sarah, I'm so glad. That's the best wedding present I could have had."

"And the city's dropping its complaint, too. Since we're not paying you anything, they've decided we're not in violation of any zoning code."

"That's fantastic. Anything more?"

She could hear Billy's murmurings in the background as Sarah said, "Hush. I'm not going to tell her that. She'll find out soon enough."

"Please. You've got to tell her," Billy urged. "She'll want to know."

"Tell me what?" Tina finally demanded.

Sarah sighed. "Samantha Junior had kittens," she said, just as Drew picked up the extension. "Five of them."

"Oh my Lord!" Drew exclaimed.

"Drew Landry!" Sarah scolded.

"Sorry."

"And," Sarah began.

"There's more?" Tina said as Drew began to sneeze in what could only be a reflex action. Those cats were thousands of miles away.

"Well, it's nothing for you to worry about, dear."

"Sarah!"

"It's just that Mr. Parsons—"

"From the board of directors?"

"Of course, dear."

"What about him?"

"He was over the other day visiting."

"Mr. Parsons was visiting? You must mean spying. He was probably looking for the germicidal warfare lab."

"I don't think so. He just wanted to make sure your wedding took place as scheduled. He seemed genuinely concerned after what happened before. And..."

"And what?" Tina said, not at all sure she wanted to hear the rest. She recognized that tone.

"Well, the poor man seemed very lonely. I mean his wife died years ago and he's all alone in the world. I think that's why he's so cranky, and he certainly was drinking way more than was good for him. We could all see that in New York. You could see it, too, couldn't you, dear?"

"What's your point, Sarah?"

Sarah was not about to be rushed. "He looked awfully pale. I doubt if he'd been eating properly either," she added as if it were a clincher. "You should have seen how thrilled he was when I asked him to stay for pot roast."

An awful premonition raced through Tina. "Sarah, you didn't," she exclaimed. "Tell me you didn't ask that man to live with us."

"But there are all these empty rooms here. It seems such a waste not to use them. And he's a fine gin rummy player."

"Sarah, I want to hear you deny it. Tell me you didn't ask him."

"Well, I didn't exactly ask. It just sort of happened. I mean we all agreed something had to be done."

Drew was chuckling on the extension.

"Drew Landry, don't you dare laugh," Tina ordered.

"I can't help it."

"I'll get you for that, Drew. I'll let Billy keep every one of those kittens," she warned, slamming down the phone. She went into the bedroom just as he was saying goodbye to Sarah. He was still chuckling. She advanced on him with a murderous expression in her bright amber eyes.

"Just think," he said cheerfully, "now we can hold the board meetings right in the living room between Scrabble games."

She dove into the middle of the bed and tackled him, pinning him down. "You...you..." Then she started laughing, too, and leaned down to kiss him. "I love you."

"You know, Mrs. Landry, life with you will never be dull."

"And even if it is," she said with a devilish glint in her eyes, "you'll have all those other people to keep you company."

Drew sobered instantly as a horrified expression flitted across his face. "Don't tell me you actually expect me to live in that house, when I have a perfectly lovely *empty* house next door."

Tina's eyes widened innocently. "You want to be alone with me?"

"Damn right."

"Why?"

"Let me show you, and we'll see if you still want to live in the middle of that mayhem at your place."

An hour later, Drew murmured, "Well, what do you think?"

"I think I'm beginning to see your point. Do you have any other arguments you'd like to try?"

He had several, each more exquisitely sensual than the last. By the time they flew home, Tina was convinced.

Besides, if she had her way, they'd fill the bedrooms in that house in no time, too. Nine or ten months from now seemed about the right time to start. She knew Sarah and Seth would approve.

In fact, she had a suspicion they were already busy wallpapering a nursery just in case.

*   *   *   *   *

**For the millions who can't read
Give the Gift of Literacy**

One out of five adults in North America
cannot read or write well enough
to fill out a job application
or understand the directions on a bottle of medicine.

**You can change all this by joining the fight
against illiteracy.**

For more information write to:
Contact, Box 81826, Lincoln, Neb. 68501
In the United States, call toll free: 1-800-228-8813

**The only degree you need
is a degree of caring**

Silhouette Special Edition

COMING NEXT MONTH

#427 LOCAL HERO—Nora Roberts
Divorcée Hester Wallace was wary of men, but her overly friendly
neighbor wasn't taking the hint. Though cartoonist Mitch Dempsey
enthralled her young son, convincing Hester to believe in heroes again was
another story entirely.

#428 SAY IT WITH FLOWERS—Andrea Edwards
Nurse Cristin O'Leary's clowning kept sick children happy, but her
response to hospital hunk Dr. Sam Rossi was no joke. Would the
handsome heart specialist have a remedy for a lovesick nurse?

#429 ARMY DAUGHTER—Maggi Charles
Architect Kerry Gundersen was no longer a lowly sergeant, but to him,
interior designer Jennifer Smith would always be the general's daughter.
As she decorated his mansion, resentment simmered . . . and desire flared
out of control.

#430 CROSS MY HEART—Phyllis Halldorson
Senator Sterling couldn't let a family scandal jeopardize his reelection;
he'd have to investigate his rascally brother's latest heartthrob. To his
chagrin, he felt his _own_ heart throbbing at his very first glimpse of her. . . .

#431 NEPTUNE SUMMER—Jeanne Stephens
Single parent Andrea Darnell knew Joe Underwood could breathe new life
into Neptune, Nebraska, but she hadn't expected mouth-to-mouth
resuscitation! Besides, did Joe really want _her_, or just her ready-made
family?

#432 GREEK TO ME—Jennifer West
Kate Reynolds's divorce had shattered her heart, and no island romance
could mend it. Still, dashing Greek Andreas Pateras was a powerful
charmer, and he'd summoned the gods to help topple Kate's resistance!

AVAILABLE NOW: